THE NOVEL AS INVESTIGATION:
LEONARDO SCIASCIA, DACIA MARAINI,
AND ANTONIO TABUCCHI

JOANN CANNON

The Novel as Investigation:
Leonardo Sciascia, Dacia Maraini,
and Antonio Tabucchi

UNIVERSITY OF TORONTO PRESS
Toronto Buffalo London

© University of Toronto Press Incorporated 2006
Toronto Buffalo London
Printed in Canada

ISBN-10: 0-8020-9114-8
ISBN-13: 978-0-8020-9114-7

Printed on acid-free paper
Toronto Italian Studies

Library and Archives Canada Cataloguing in Publication

Cannon, JoAnn
    The novel as investigation : Leonardo Sciascia, Dacia Maraini, and
Antonio Tabucchi / JoAnn Cannon.

(Toronto Italian studies)
Includes bibliographical references and index.
ISBN-13: 978-0-8020-9114-7
ISBN-10: 0-8020-9114-8

1. Sciascia, Leonardo.   2. Maraini, Dacia.   3. Tabucchi, Antonio, 1943–.
4. Detective and mystery stories, Italian – History and criticism.
I. Title.   II. Series.

PQ4181.D4C36 2006   853'.0872'090914   C2006-900552-4

This book has been published with the assistance of a grant from the Division of Humanities, Arts and Cultural Studies and the Office of Research, University of California, Davis.

University of Toronto Press acknowledges the financial assistance to its publishing program of the Canada Council for the Arts and the Ontario Arts Council.

University of Toronto Press acknowledges the financial support for its publishing activities of the Government of Canada through the Book Publishing Industry Development Program (BPIDP).

To Bob and Matt

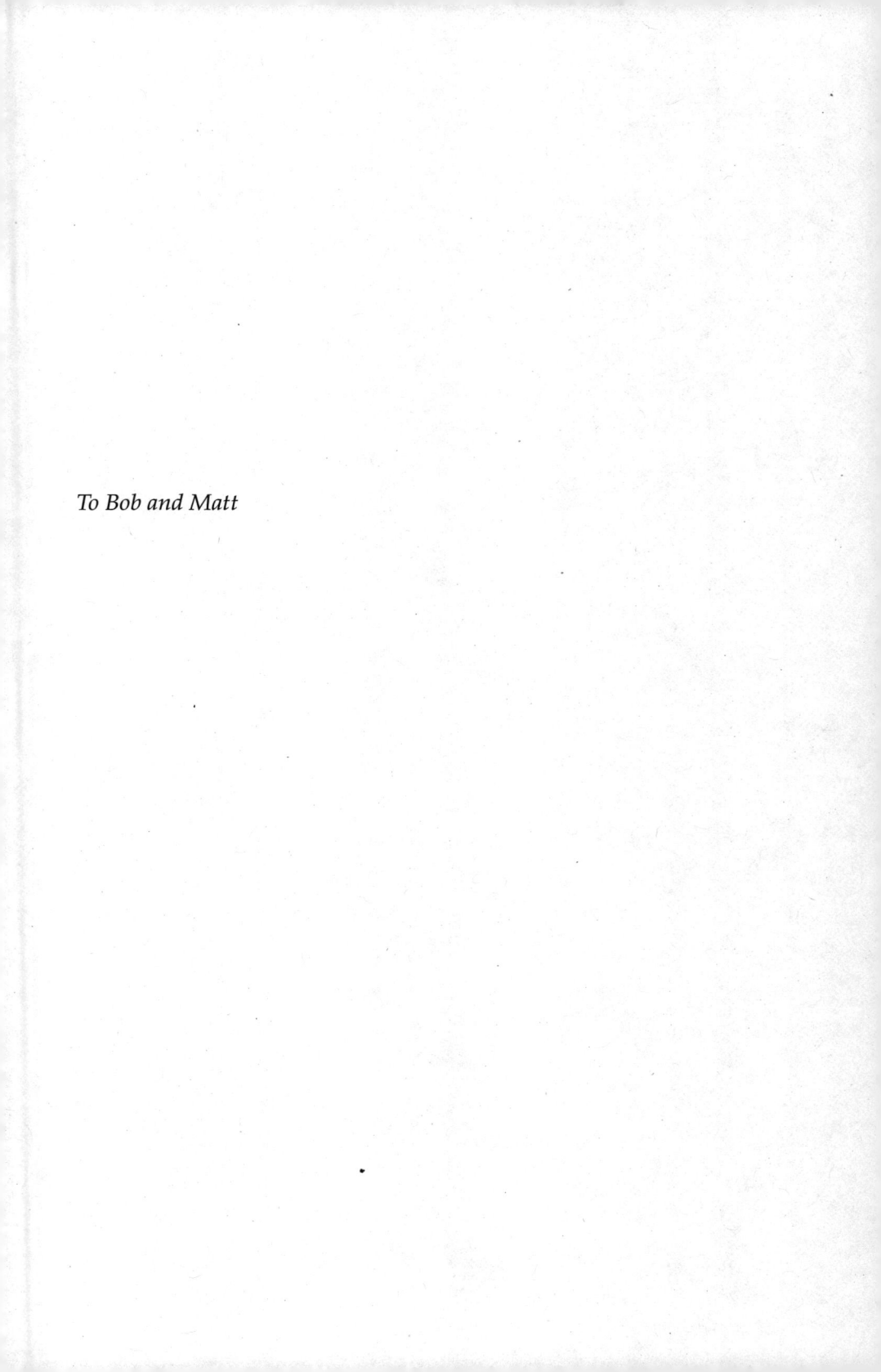

Contents

Acknowledgments ix

Introduction   3

1 The Power of the Pen in Leonardo Sciascia's *Porte aperte*   17

2 The Death of the Detective in *Il cavaliere e la morte*   31

3 In Search of Isolina   45

4 *Voci* and the Conventions of the *Giallo*   59

5 Ethics and Literature in *Sostiene Pereira: Una testimonianza*   73

6 Detection, Activism, and Writing in *La testa perduta di Damasceno Monteiro*   87

Conclusion   101

Notes   107

Bibliography   123

Index   131

Acknowledgments

I would like to express my heartfelt appreciation to Dacia Maraini, for her hospitality while I was in Rome and for her willingness to share her insights with our students at the University of California, Davis, during two visits to northern California sponsored by the Istituto italiano di cultura. Many thanks to Antonio Tabucchi for the pleasure of his company at a lively luncheon in Pisa and to Lorenzo Greco for organizing this congenial gathering. I would also like to express my gratitude to the American Academy in Rome for the opportunity to work on this project as a visiting scholar in the spring of 2004 and to the National Endowment for the Humanities and other foundations for their support of the American Academy. I am indebted to the many undergraduate and graduate students, in particular Shawn Doubiago, Andy Matt, and Loredana Giacalone, with whom I have discussed the works of Maraini, Tabucchi, and Sciascia and whose insights and curiosity have stimulated my thinking over the past few years; and to Charles Klopp for his insight and suggestions. Finally, I extend a special note of thanks to Ron Schoeffel at the University of Toronto Press for his encouragement and support.

An earlier version of chapter 4 appeared as '*Voci* and the Conventions of the *Giallo*' in *Italica* 78 (Summer 2001): 193–203, and chapter 6 was published as 'Detection, Activism and Writing in Tabucchi's *La testa perduta di Damasceno Monteiro*' in *Quaderni d'italianistica* 23, no. 1 (2002): 163–72. I wish to thank the respective editors of these journals for publishing my work and for granting permission to reprint it here.

THE NOVEL AS INVESTIGATION:
LEONARDO SCIASCIA, DACIA MARAINI,
AND ANTONIO TABUCCHI

Introduction

Leonardo Sciascia, Dacia Maraini, Antonio Tabucchi. Key works of these three Italian novelists, from the mid-1980s to the end of the century, intersect in striking and significant ways, arriving at a similar juncture at approximately the same point in time. This book will examine a series of these works that focus on crime and punishment, justice and injustice, testimony and judgment: *Porte aperte* (1985) and *Il cavaliere e la morte* (1989) by Sciascia, *Isolina* (1985) and *Voci* (1994) by Maraini, and *Sostiene Pereira* (1994) and *La testa perduta di Damasceno Monteiro* (1997) by Tabucchi. Each of these texts, whether a detective novel or a *racconto d'inchiesta* (investigative novel), is a work in which investigation or inquiry is the driving force. The inquiry is undertaken by a range of closely related character types: non-professional detectives, police investigators, lawyers, judges, and crusading journalists. All of the texts in question shed light on pressing social ills: Sciascia focuses on abuses of power and the death penalty, Maraini on violence against women, Tabucchi on torture, police brutality, and human rights violations. The protagonists of the works in question – a radio journalist in 1990s Rome, a crusading lawyer in contemporary Lisbon, a judge in fascist Italy of the thirties, the editor of the cultural pages of a newspaper in fascist Portugal – have one common trait: they all suffer for what Elio Vittorini calls in *Conversazione in Sicilia* 'il male del mondo offeso' (the woes of the outraged world). Indeed, the problems explored in these texts are not specific to Italian society of the late twentieth century but are, unfortunately, universal in scope. This study explores each writer's denunciation of social injustice and indictment of the guilty party in complementary texts, one group set in present-day society (*Il cavaliere e la morte*, *Voci*, *La testa perduta di Damasceno*

Monteiro), the other in a past that continues to inform the present moment (*Porte aperte, Isolina, Sostiene Pereira*). Sciascia, Maraini, and Tabucchi share a strong conviction of the power of narrative in society, and all three writers self-reflexively explore that power within their literary texts. As an extension of this conviction of the power of the pen, each writer focuses on the role of reading within the texts in question and examines some aspect of the reading process in his or her fiction.

Leonardo Sciascia made his literary debut in 1956 with *Le parrocchie di Regalpetra*, a fictionalized account of life in his native Racalmuto. With the publication of his detective novels of the sixties and early seventies, Sciascia came to be recognized as one of Italy's most engaging and significant writers. The detective genre perfectly captures Sciascia's *forma mentis*. His work is situated between two poles, belief in the exercise of reason as symbolized in the *giallo* (detective novel) and dismay at the defeat of reason and the prevalence of injustice in the world. *Il giorno della civetta* (1961), his first detective novel, is an indictment of the Sicilian mafia and of corruption at the highest level of the Italian government. The protagonist, Captain Bellodi, a northern Italian and former partisan, succeeds in solving the mystery and linking the hitman to the *capomafia* and his influential connections in the Italian government. Although the pervasiveness of the mafia is fully exposed in the novel, the author withholds any unrealistic, happy ending in which the guilty are brought to justice or the mafia is eradicated. *Il giorno* was followed by *A ciascuno il suo* (1966), in which the guilty not only remain unpunished, but truth is silenced through the brutal murder of the amateur detective, Professor Laurana. *Il contesto* (1971), Sciascia's third detective novel, is a parody of the Italian political scene of the seventies, and in particular an indictment of the *compromesso storico* (historic compromise) between the Christian Democratic Party and the Italian Communist Party. The novel is an attack on the blurring of ideological distinctions among the myriad political parties of Italy's *partitocrazia* and the struggle for political power at all costs. *Il contesto* is set in an unnamed country described in the author's note in terms that condemn the Italian political scene of the 1970s: 'dove non avevano più corso le idee, dove i principi – ancora proclamati e conclamati – venivano quotidianamente irrisi, dove le ideologie si riducevano in politica a pure denominazioni nel giuoco delle parti che il potere si assegnava, dove soltanto il potere per il potere contava' (121) [an entirely imaginary country: a country where ideas no longer circulate, where principles – still proclaimed, still acclaimed – are made a daily mockery, where ideologies are reduced to policies in name only, in a party-politics game in which only power for the sake of power counts] (*Equal Danger*, 118–19).[1] In his early detective novels, whether set in Sicily or in unnamed countries that bear a striking resemblance to Italy, Sciascia targets both the Sicilian mafia and the larger mafia of power politics in Italy. With *Todo modo* (1974) he focuses his attention on the struggle between scepticism and absolutism as embodied in the Catholic Church.[2] After a period from the late seventies to the middle eighties in which he abandoned fiction in favour of documentary prose, Sciascia began to write several works of fiction that mark a turning point in his career.[3] These include *1912 +1*, *Porte aperte*, and *Il cavaliere e la morte*. By this point, at what proved to be the end of the author's life, his focus seems to have shifted from current political and social problems of Italy to questions of an ethical and even spiritual dimension. As Joseph Farrell has convincingly pointed out in his study of Sciascia's last works, 'At the heart of these works is an eschatological quest not found in the early Sciascia, but of a type common in the mature work of many European writers' (140). It is on these texts, particulary *Porte aperte* (1988) and *Il cavaliere e la morte* (1989), written in the last two years of the author's life, that this study will focus.[4]

Porte aperte, set in fascist Italy in 1937, is the story of a judge called upon to preside over the trial of a triple murderer. The fascist regime expects to see the crime, in which one of the victims was a high-ranking fascist functionary, punished with the death penalty. The judge not only firmly opposes the use of the death penalty, but also ridicules the notion that Italians may sleep safely with open doors (the 'porte aperte' of the title) under fascist rule. Chapter 1 of this study will examine the judge's courageous refusal to comply with fascist authority. The judge's decision is based less on an ideological position than on an ethical foundation informed largely by reading. I will examine the way in which Sciascia dramatizes the weight of the written word as an effective form of opposition to oppressive power. *Porte aperte* becomes one element of a long indictment of capital punishment by writers ranging from Montaigne and Beccaria to Tolstoy and Dostoievsky.

Like the novels of the sixties and early seventies that established Leonardo Sciascia's literary reputation, *Il cavaliere e la morte*, his penultimate novel, takes the familiar form of the *giallo*. The protagonist, a police investigator known only as the deputy, is investigating what will prove to be his final case. Chapter 2 will focus on the way in which

Sciascia exploits the detective novel format not to shed light on a specifically Sicilian or Italian problem, as in his early detective novels, but rather to dramatize the universality of the never-ending struggle against the corruption of absolute power. The president of a large corporation, United Industries, is responsible for the murder of a lawyer who had uncovered far-reaching corruption in the president's organization. The protagonist quickly and expeditiously solves the crime and identifies the guilty party, but is powerless to bring the influential culprit to justice. The focus of the novel falls less on the murder investigation and more on the character of the deputy, who bears a strong resemblance to Leonardo Sciascia himself. Written shortly before Sciascia's death in 1989, the novel not only tells the story of the deputy's investigation but also relates the thoughts on life and death, justice and injustice, of a dying man. Reflecting Sciascia's final thoughts as he lays down his pen, *Il cavaliere e la morte* is a vehicle to explore the power of writing, reading, and rereading to combat injustice. The knight of the Durer engraving *The Knight, Death, and the Devil* comes to symbolize the figure of the writer and the power of the pen.

Dacia Maraini, long known as one of Italy's foremost feminist writers, has also been one of that nation's most visible and active public intellectuals from the 1960s to the present day.[5] Maraini began her literary career in the early sixties.[6] In such novels as *La vacanza* (1962), *L'età del malessere* (1963), *Donna in guerra* (1975), *Dialogo di una prostituta con un suo cliente* (1976), and *Il treno per Helsinki* (1984), and in her plays from *Il manifesto* (1969) to *Maria Stuarda* to *Veronica Franca, meretrice e scrittora* (1992), she has dealt with the lives of women in all walks of life, from the prison convict to the prostitute to the lower-class salesgirl to the upper-middle-class professional. *La lunga vita di Marianna Ucrìa* (1994) signalled her shift away from contemporary characters and 'timely' social issues towards historical fiction. The novel, set against the backdrop of the unenlightened Sicily of the eighteenth century, presents the trajectory of the life of a Sicilian noblewoman and deaf mute. Maraini deftly traces the writing of the female destiny by patriarchal society and explores the issue of violence against women.

With *Isolina* (1985) and *Voci* (1994) Maraini uses two complementary genres, the detective novel and the *racconto d'inchiesta*, to continue to explore the issue of violence against women. In *Isolina*, the author meticulously reconstructs a forgotten chapter of history, an actual unsolved murder in turn-of-the-century Verona. Chapter 3 of this work, on *Isolina*, will explore the way in which the author/historian signals her presence in the history as she assembles the puzzle and fills in the gaps in the historical record. I will argue that Maraini's successful crusade to bring the story to light is an example of ethical interpretation in history in which the object of study is not history or the past, but 'the social matrix ... as an extension of the past into the writer's present' (White, 305). I will underscore the author's presence in the process of writing Isolina's untold story and show how this lays bare the power of the pen in action.

While *Isolina* is a reconstruction of a murder case in the first year of the twentieth century, *Voci* is a fictional *giallo* set in contemporary Italy. *Voci* focuses on crimes against women at two levels. The protagonist, a radio journalist, investigates the murder of her neighbour while simultaneously exploring the issue of unsolved crimes against women for her radio station. Chapter 4 will show how Maraini both exploits and overturns the norms of detective fiction to expose one of the most troubling scourges of contemporary society. While the protagonist solves the Angela Bari case, the larger crime of violence against women continues unabated. With her open-ended conclusion Maraini points her finger at patriarchal society itself as the guilty party. The final page of *Voci*, where the protagonist entertains the possibility of writing the story we have just finished reading, represents a meta-narrative comment on the efficacy of the written word as a weapon in the battle against injustice.

Antonio Tabucchi began his literary career in the mid-1970s with the historical novel *Piazza d'Italia*.[7] That novel, focusing as it does on three generations of an Italian peasant family, anarchists, antifascists, and communists, is a kind of micro-history of Italy's oppressed from the unification to the present.[8] Tabucchi then proceeded to write what has been considered largely postmodern, fantastic fiction, from *Il gioco del rovescio* (1981) to *Notturno indiano* (1984) to *I volatili di Beato Angelico* (1987) to *Requiem* (1991).[9] As Charles Klopp has noted, however, the focus on Tabucchi's postmodernism has distracted attention from 'the specifically ethical nature of the themes that run through his books' ('Antonio Tabucchi,' 332). In the early nineties, this 'ethical' element in Tabucchi's narrative began to come to the forefront. With the publication of *Sostiene Pereira* (1994), his work took a turn towards what has been called a literature of 'impegno civile.'[10] One of the first reviewers of *Sostiene Pereira* welcomed the novel as heralding a turn away from the 'letteraria e raffinata' (the literary and refined) and towards 'una tematica più impegnata (more politically committed themes).'[11] In this

8 The Novel as Investigation

study I will focus on *Sostiene Pereira*, set in 1930s fascist Portugal, and *La testa perduta di Damasceno Monteiro* (1997).

Chapter 5 will consider *Sostiene Pereira: Una testimonianza*. Widely acclaimed upon its publication in 1994, *Sostiene Pereira* examines the gradual 'presa di coscienza' of a Portuguese journalist writing in Lisbon in 1938. The author not only deals with ethical questions in the novel, but also focuses on the ethics of reading and writing. In *Sostiene Pereira* the young revolutionary and Pereira's collaborator draws his inspiration from writers like Garcia Lorca, while his mentor, Pereira, publishes a translation of Daudet's 'La dernière class' as a recognition of the way in which literature may subvert authoritarian regimes. I will examine how Tabucchi's novel raises a series of questions being asked by writers and critics whose work is taking an 'ethical turn,' and argues for the importance of an ethically engaged literature.

Tabucchi's *La testa perduta di Damasceno Monteiro* is a murder mystery featuring an idealistic journalist and a crusading lawyer. An unidentified young man is found murdered and decapitated on the banks of the Douro River in Oporto. The guilty party proves to be a corrupt, drug-dealing sergeant in the Portuguese Guardia Nacional. This case of police brutality, torture, and murder, based upon an actual crime in the mid-1990s in Lisbon, is solved midway through the novel. Indeed, Tabucchi's 'fictional' solution anticipated the outcome of the actual case, in which a corrupt police sergeant was ultimately convicted of the crime. Tabucchi draws upon the detective genre in part, at least, to expose and denounce torture and police brutality, injustices that know no national boundaries. The text not only recounts the attempt to bring the guilty party to justice; as I will demonstrate in Chapter 6, much of *La testa perduta* explores the role of writing in society. Tabucchi's defence of literature, including but not limited to writing that is disruptive to the existing social order, intersects with similar self-reflexive comments on the capabilities and responsibilities of literature by Sciascia and Maraini.

These three diverging literary careers intersect at the point in the mid-1980s at which this study begins. Each of the texts examined in this volume highlights an injustice and an investigator who is committed to exposing that injustice. Indeed, each of these writers views his or her work as both an investigation and a mode of inquiry. In a 1996 interview, Dacia Maraini comments on the cognitive thrust that informs her work:

Per me il motore, la spinta a scrivere nasce sempre da un desiderio conoscitivo. Sono attratta da un tema, o meglio da un personaggio, che può rappresentare e contenere un tema, che mi spinge a conoscere meglio una certa realtà, che può essere psicologica, sociale, storica. E' sempre una spinta conoscitiva, io scrivo un racconto per cercare di capire meglio qualcosa che ... mi interessa. (Wright, 78)[12]

[For me the impulse to write is always born of a cognitive desire. I am attracted by a theme, or rather by a character who may represent and contain a theme, which pushes me to understand better a certain psychological, social or historical reality. It is always a question of a cognitive impulse. I write a story in order to understand better something that ... interests me.][13]

Later in the interview Maraini refers to both *Isolina: la donna tagliata a pezzi* and *Voci* as texts that are informed by this same 'necessità conoscitiva' (89).

Antonio Tabucchi defines writing in similar terms. In *La gastrite di Platone* Tabucchi passionately defends the 'funzione interrogativa' of the writer.[14] In a 1995 interview entitled 'Dove va il romanzo?' Tabucchi suggests: 'si scrive anche per una ragione ultima che forse è una soluzione, una condanna' [one writes for a reason which is, ultimately, a solution, a condemnation]. Later in the interview the author discusses the relation between the detective novel and his recent fiction. In response to a question about the narrative structure of *Sostiene Pereira*, Tabucchi comments on the inspiration he has derived from the detective genre:

Per la prima volta ... mi sono confrontato con una letteratura interrogativa, quella gialla, che io amo molto sia nella sua forma più popolare – i gialli che escono settimanalmente – che in quelle di alto livello letterario come potrebbero essere i 'gialli' scritti da Sciascia o da Durrenmatt. Ho poi utilizzato questo modello anche in *Pereira*, che in fondo è un romanzo giallo ... modellato ... secondo quel motivo di ricerca e di interrogazione che è caratteristico della letteratura poliziesca. (*Conversazione*, 19–20)

[For the first time ... I confronted interrogative literature, detective fiction, which I love both in its popular form – the detective stories that come out weekly – and in those highly literary detective stories like the *gialli* written by Sciascia or Durrenmatt. I used this model also in *Pereira*, which is fundamentally a detective novel, patterned on that motif of research and interrogation which is characteristic of detective fiction.]

Not surprisingly, Tabucchi cites Sciascia as the writer whose works most clearly epitomize the 'motivo di ricerca e di interrogazione' of the narrative he both admires and emulates. Sciascia himself has recognized the investigative thrust to all his writing, whether detective fiction, historical novel, or historical essay. The author views his writing as a form of detection: 'Lo scrittore svela la verità decifrando la realtà e sollevandola alla superficie, in un certo senso semplificandola, anche rendendola più oscura ... Ecco perché utilizzo spesso il "discorso" del romanzo poliziesco, questa forma di resoconto che tende alla verità dei fatti e alla denuncia del colpevole' (*La Sicilia come metafora*, 87–8) [The writer uncovers the truth by deciphering reality and raising it to the surface, in a certain sense by simplifying it, even rendering it more obscure ... This is why I often adopt the 'discourse' of detective fiction, this form of writing which tends toward the truth of facts and the denunciation of the guilty party]. The six texts studied in this volume are each informed by the same investigative impulse outlined by Sciascia, Maraini, and Tabucchi both in their critical essays and interviews and in their fiction.

For each writer the investigative thrust may take the form of a *giallo*, as in *Il cavaliere e la morte*, *Voci*, and *La testa perduta di Damasceo Monteiro*, or it may instead take the form of a historical investigation, as in *Porte aperte*, *Isolina*, and *Sostiene Pereira*. The historical novels and essays of these writers exhibit many of the same characteristics as the detective novel. In each case the writer becomes a detective who uncovers and deciphers the past. Each of the authors in question uses the historical novel format not only to shed light on the past, but also to comment on the present moment.[15] Claude Ambroise has discussed the way in which Sciascia's historical *inchieste* anticipate the micro-histories of Carlo Ginzburg or Nathalie Zemon Davis. The micro-histories of the 1980s replace the 'storia ufficiale' with the history of the forgotten, the marginalized, and the vanquished. Ambroise draws one clear distinction between Sciascia's work and the studies of these micro-historians, however: 'Eppure mi sembrano diverse per due motivi. Primo: il *fait divers* del passato t'interessa perché rientra in una problematica (morale, politica) che è ancora nostra, non per l'episodio in sé' (*Opere*, 2: xxi).[16] In works like *Morte dell'Inquisitore* and *La strega e il capitano* Sciascia has indeed found occasion to look back to the past not as an archaic remnant, but as bearing the seeds of the present moment.[17] *Porte aperte* is a case in point. In the second chapter of the novel Sciascia explicitly positions his text, set in 1938 fascist Italy, in direct relationship to the 'present' (1987, the year in which the novel was written). The reader is abruptly reminded that the present must be read in relation to the past. The injustices of 1937 fascist Italy have not entirely been extinguished; capital punishment is a present-day reality.[18]

The connectedness of the historical anecdote to the present moment is also apparent in Tabucchi's historical novel. In the authorial note appended to *Sostiene Pereira* Tabucchi explains the significance of the date in which the novel is set, 1938: 'Ripensai all'Europa sull'orlo del disastro della Seconda Guerra mondiale, alla Guerra civile spagnola, alle tragedie del nostro passato *prossimo*. E nell'estate del novantatrè, quando Pereira, divenuto un mio vecchio amico, mi aveva raccontato la sua storia, io potei scriverla' (48, my emphasis) [I thought about Europe on the brink of the disaster of the Second World War, about the Spanish civil war, about all the tragedies of our *recent* past. And in the summer of 1993, when Pereira, having become an old friend of mine, told me his story, I was able to write it down]. The insistence on the proximity of the past in the qualifier 'prossimo' and the linking of 1938 to 1993 speak for themselves.[19] As Charles Klopp notes in his discussion of *Sostiene Pereira*, Tabucchi is well aware that fascism 'is not only a historical category but a perennial menace and a temptation of the spirit' ('Antonio Tabucchi,' 332).

Dacia Maraini is a writer who alternately delves into the most 'timely' of contemporary realities and resurrects chapters of women's histories unrecorded or neglected by official histories. Maraini is always in search of what she calls 'le radici più profonde della nostra cultura,'[20] whether the search for historical roots takes her to turn-of-the-century Verona (in *Isolina*), eighteenth-century Sicily (*La lunga vita di Marianna Ucrìa*), or sixteenth-century Venice (*Veronia Franca, Meretrice e scrittora*). As the author frequently reminds us, the stories of women's lives have been suppressed by history. In a 1991 interview with Serena Anderlini Maraini, responds to a question regarding Cixous's call for women to enter history. The author remarks: '*Preistoria* is characterized by an unconsciousness: letting yourself live, living by instinct, or even by reason, but a reason fairly well closed up in that particular moment. Instead, the characteristic of *storia* is reflecting on yourself at the moment you're living, while you look at yourself live. This is *storia*, which is a continuity of memory. *Preistoria* is, precisely, outside of *storia*. Its day is sufficient unto itself; it has no memory. Women are entering *storia* in our era' (159).[21] It is Maraini's project to look back to the past, to break the silence to which both men and women have contributed. *Isolina* is a case in point. Maraini's text, an accurate historical reconstruction of a forgotten episode of history, combats the kind of historical amnesia that would allow a story like Isolina's to fall into oblivion.

This study spans the period from the mid-1980s to the end of the twentieth century, a period of tremendous change and political upheaval in Italian society. Following the political turmoil of the 1970s, Italy in the mid-1980s suddenly found that it had surpassed Great Britain as the fifth largest economy in the world.[22] This unprecedented prosperity could not, however, mask some complex problems, including a large and inefficient public sector, a wide gap between rich and poor as well as north and south, and political stagnation caused by the *trasformismo* and resulting dominance of the Christian Democrats in all the coalitions of the post-war era. With the fall of the Berlin wall and the collapse of communism in Europe, the hegemony of the Christian Democrats also began to collapse. This was followed shortly by the *Mani pulite* scandal of the early 1990s. Beginning with the arrest in Milan of a Socialist Party official who had accepted a bribe in exchange for a cleaning contract for a nursing home, the scandal, often referred to as *Tangentopoli* (Bribes-ville or Bribe-gate), touched not only the Socialists but all of the major Italian political parties. As the *Economist* correspondent summarized in February 1993 (in 'The Fall of Montecitorio'): 'The confessions on which the prosecution has based its case so far have revealed a systematic imposition of kickbacks in virtually all public-sector contracts, from the construction of the Milan metro down' (45). The political system began to unravel as it was confirmed that such corruption was not only rampant throughout Italy, but was at the very basis of the old party system. As the arrests increased and the evidence mounted, the mayors of all of Italy's major cities stepped down, most in disgrace. Bettino Craxi, leader of the Socialist Party, was indicted and fled the country to avoid trial. All of the major political parties, the Christian Democrats, Communists, and Socialists, were implicated in the scandal. Giulio Andreotti, the 'elder statesman' of the Christian Democratic Party, was indicted on charges of being a member of the mafia.

> The sheer extent of Tangentopoli – taking in over thirty other 'bribe cities' apart from Milan – was beyond the belief of even well-informed *aficionados*. More than 1000 politicians and business figures were, by March 1993, under investigation. Tens of thousands of party bureaucrats were implicated. The parliamentary immunity against prosecution of 75 Deputies and Senators had been lifted. Large swathes of public administration and private industry had functioned in a distorted market of entry fees, commissions, inflated costs and reduced competition. (Bufacchi and Burgess, 120)

Eventually the downfall of all the governing parties led to a new era. As Umberto Eco remarked in his February 1993 *Espresso* column: 'We are living ... through our own 14th of July 1789.'[23] The formation of new political parties combined with reconfigurations of the old governing parties. The Italian Communist party regrouped as two parties, the Partitio democratico di sinistra and Rifondazione comunista. The defunct Christian Democratic Party split into the centre-left Italian Popular Party and two centre-right parties. The rise of the Forza Italia movement headed by Silvio Berlusconi dates to this period.[24]

While Sciascia did not live to see the collapse of the old political landscape in Italy, he certainly chronicled much of the corruption that led to the eventual downfall of the old order. Maraini and Tabucchi were of course eye witnesses to the fall of the post-war political system. Whether their fictions were directly affected by the political upheaval of the period is perhaps beside the point. Some critics have read the Italian fiction of the last two decades of the twentieth century as emerging from a widespread sense of political apathy in Italy.[25] Others suggest that the indifference to politics of the 1980s known as the *riflusso* was replaced by a renewed engagement in politics during the 1990s as old political parties collapsed and new ones emerged from the ashes.[26] It is not the purpose of my study to explore the political persuasions of individual writers. Suffice it to say that, in a political context characterized as much by stagnation and scandal as by renewal, it is not surprising that each of the writers studied in this volume has continued to engage in political activity while showing a certain healthy scepticism towards politics. Certainly each of these writers avoids the prescription of political solutions in his or her writing. The texts highlighted in this study cannot be read as *letteratura impegnata*, politically committed literature, in the dogmatic sense in which that term was used during the immediate post-war period.[27]

The political context in which the neo-realist works emerged was one of much greater euphoria than the late twentieth century in Italy.[28] The works studied in this volume are characterized by an engagement with society through an ethical rather than a political stance. The ethical thrust of the final works of Sciascia, and the recent work of Tabucchi and Maraini, some of the most significant Italian fiction of the late twentieth century, is one of the subjects of this study.

Sciascia, Maraini, and Tabucchi do not belong to a particular literary 'school' or current. Yet there are striking family resemblances among these three writers' works that the present study will attempt to trace. The points of contact have been commented on by the writers themselves. Both Maraini and Tabucchi began to recognize Leonardo Sciascia as a kindred spirit during the period studied in this volume. Tabucchi dedicated his 1998 book on the role of the intellectual, *La gastrite di Platone*, to the memory of Leonardo Sciascia and Pier Paolo Pasolini.[29] Maraini, when asked in an interview about her relationship to Sciascia, acknowledged their kinship: 'Sciascia è siciliano come me. Abbiamo tutti e due una curiosità isolana, che ci spinge a frugare nella realtà' (Sciascia is Sicilian like me. We both have a Sicilian curiosity that drives us to delve into reality) (Debenedetti, 00). She has expressed great sympathy for Sciascia's work over the years, and particularly admired the feminist sensibilities of Sciascia's 1986 *La strega e il capitano*.[30] As concerns the relationship between Maraini and Tabucchi, in a heartfelt note to a recent monograph on Tabucchi, Maraini remarks on the fond memories she has of various encounters with Tabucchi over the years. Each time their conversations have focused on two subjects: books and their mutual 'civic passions' (*passioni civili*). She closes by thanking Tabucchi for his constant readiness to 'denunciare una inguistizia.'[31]

One of the most striking points of contact between *Porte aperte*, *Il cavaliere e la morte*, *Sostiene Pereira*, *La testa perduta*, *Isolina*, and *Voci* is the way in which they more or less explicitly and self-reflexively explore the role to be played by writing, the power of the pen. Sciascia, Maraini, and Tabucchi share a strong notion of the social and moral responsibility of literature. The ethical 'nourishment' to be gained from reading is shown to be no less important than the act of taking up the pen. Both Sciascia and Tabucchi take pains to outline the contribution of reading to the ethical formation of the character. Leonardo Sciascia's *Porte aperte* is a case in point. The character of the judge, an authorial surrogate, is a literate and literary man. The ethical foundation on which the judge builds his opposition to the death penalty is constructed from a wide range of literary sources, from Dostoievsky to Beccaria to Leopardi. The protagonist of Sciascia's *Il cavaliere e la morte*, whose bookshelf includes Montaigne, Verga, Stevenson, Gadda, Tolstoy, Borges, Gogol, and Hugo, is cast in the same mold. Similarly, Tabucchi features protagonists whose decisions and actions are guided by literary sources. In *Sostiene Pereira*, the young revolutionary and Pereira's collaborator draws his inspiration from writers like Garcia Lorca, while his mentor, Pereira, publishes a translation of Daudet's 'La dernière class' as a recognition of the way in which literature may subvert authoritarian regimes. In *La testa perduta di Damasceno Monteiro*, the crusading lawyer, Loton, instructs his protégé, the young journalist Firmino, on the value of literature. Not only does Loton urge the importance of socially committed works of non-fiction such as Alleg's denunciation of torture in *The Question*; he also defends the importance of a wide and eclectic range of fiction by such authors as Colet, Gide, Vittorini, and Flaubert. In Maraini's *Voci* the power of the pen is dramatized on the last page of the novel when Michela, having been relieved of her journalistic assignment, considers the possibility of writing a book on unsolved crimes against women (a novel that coincides with the text we have just read). For Maraini's protagonist, reading narratives also serves as a cognitive tool. Literary works from fairy tales to Conrad's *Secret Sharer* give the detective the necessary tools to unlock the mystery of the Angela Bari murder case and to solve the crime.

The present study might be read as characteristic of the recent ethical turn in literary studies.[32] My approach focuses largely on ethical thematics and on what Buell calls 'the underlying value commitments of literary texts and their implied authors' (7). I must acknowledge that I have been led in this direction by the authors themselves. The texts in question lend themselves to and even invite this type of ethically valenced critical approach. The detective novels and the *racconti d'inchiesta* of Sciascia, Maraini, and Tabucchi indeed are genres subtended by an ethos in which reason, justice, truth, testimony, and judgment are highly valued and valorized. Each of the texts in question self-reflexively explores the relation between ethics and literature, as well as the ethics of reading. Like many critics whose work has taken an ethical turn, I myself have not grounded my inquiry in a specific ethical model. Rather, I have engaged in a close reading in the interest of allowing the texts themselves to reflect self-consciously upon the ethical values of their implied authors.

1 The Power of the Pen in Leonardo Sciascia's *Porte Aperte*

Leonardo Sciascia's credentials as a historian have been evident throughout his literary career. In such works as *Morte dell'Inquisitore*, *La strega e il capitano*, and *La scomparsa di Majorana*, Sciascia delves into unexplored chapters of Italian history. *Morte dell'Inquisitore*, a text inspired by Manzoni's *Storia della colonna infame*, reconstructs the story of the Augustinian monk who, persecuted by the Inquisition for political and not religious 'heresies,' retaliated by assassinating his inquisitor.[1] The book is a historical detective novel in which the author searches for every available scrap of evidence in order to reconstruct the historical record as accurately as possible. The same meticulous archival research is evident in *La strega e il capitano* (1986), published in celebration of the bicentenary of Manzoni's birth. Sciascia takes his departure from a brief reference in the thirty-first chapter of *I promessi sposi* to a sixteenth-century persecution of one Caterina Medici, accused of witchcraft, tortured, strangled, and burned by the Inquisition. The author reconstructs the story of this miscarriage of justice in what Dacia Maraini has hailed as Sciascia's first feminist text. Each of these chapters of history represents an abuse of power in which the law is enlisted in the service not of justice and truth but of injustice and falsehood. Throughout his work it is evident that Sciascia found the key to the present in the past, whether the near past of the fascist regime or the distant past of the Inquisition.[2] Even the detective novels, *Il giorno della civetta*, *A ciascuno il suo*, *Il contesto*, and *Todo modo*, set either in present-day Sicily and Italy or in unnamed modern European cities, all contain frequent references to the ever-present past.

With his 1987 *Porte aperte* Leonardo Sciascia turns back the clock by fifty years. *Porte aperte* is loosely based on an incident that occurred in

Palermo in 1937. Unlike *Morte dell'Inquisitore* or *La strega e il capitano*, scrupulously faithful to the historical record in the tradition of Manzoni's *Storia della colonna infame*, *Porte aperte* is a historical novel, a 'componimento misto di storia e fantasia.'[3] The novel explores what Sciascia regards as one of the most despicable crimes of the fascist regime, and of our present moment: the imposition of the death penalty. The title refers to the allegedly heightened sense of security that allowed the Italian people to sleep with 'open doors' following the fascist regime' the re-establishment of the death penalty. As the author explains, the novel was inspired by an actual event: 'E un episodio realmente accaduto a Palermo che io però ho trattato con molta libertà. C'è un magistrato che, chiamato a giudicare su un delitto, si rifiuta di infliggere la pena di morte ... Tutto si svolge nel '37' (*Opere*, 3:xlii)[4] [It is an event which actually happened in Palermo but with which however, I took great liberties. There is a magistrate who, called upon to judge a crime, refuses to inflict the death penalty ... It all takes place in 37]. A man is accused of the brutal and premeditated murder of three victims: his wife, his employer, and the accountant hired to replace him in the employer's firm after his embezzlement has been discovered. The employer, a certain Avvocato Bruno, is a high-ranking fascist functionary. The sentence expected by the powers-that-be is preordained. Both the severity of the crime and the fascist affiliations of one of the victims leave no room for mercy: 'aspettano una sentenza sbrigativa ed esemplare' *(Opere*, 3:333) [They expect a swift, exemplary sentence] (*Open Doors*, 12). The judge's principled stand against capital punishment is expressed not only in word but in deed, as he refuses to impose the expected sentence at the conclusion of the novel.

The focus of Sciascia's *Porte aperte* is not on the solution of the crime, the course of the trial, or the question of innocence or guilt of the accused. The novel investigates a broader issue: the noxious effects of the death penalty on civil society. The protagonist fully recognizes the political nature of the death penalty as a means of consolidating power, in this case fascist power. In the opening scene of the novel the protagonist, referred to as the 'little judge,' discusses with his superior, the prosecutor, the case about to come before the court. Recalling the conversation they had ten years prior on the occasion of the re-establishment of the death penalty by the fascist regime, the prosecutor expresses his concern that the judge may not be able to handle the case. The prosecutor advises the judge, who staunchly denounced the death penalty ten years prior, to reroute the case to another court. Given the status of one of the victims in the fascist regime, this is the safe course of action. The judge declines to take the prosecutor's advice, and instead counters with his denunciation of the death penalty and reconfirms his earlier opposition to capital punishment. 'Consideri, poi, se gli istinti che ribollono in un linciaggio, il furore, la follia, non siano, in definitiva, di minore atrocità del macabro rito che promuove una corte di giustizia dando sentenza di morte' (*Opere,* 3:336) [But surely the instincts that erupt in a lynching, the fury and madness, are less atrocious than the macabre ritual that activates a court of justice in pronouncing the death sentence]' (*Open Doors,* 15). The normally taciturn judge continues his diatribe against the death penalty with uncharacteristic eloquence, while the prosecutor advances the 'porte aperte' argument in favour of capital punishment. Citing the diminished crime rate since the re-establishment of the death penalty ten years prior, the prosecutor reminds the judge that the Italian people may now sleep with open doors. The judge dismisses the conventional wisdom and responds laconically, 'Io chiudo sempre le mie' (*Opere,* 3:337) [I always close mine] (*Open Doors,* 17). The character of the judge, and the judge's character, begin to emerge in this opening dialogue. The exchange between the protagonist and his superior sets the stage for the drama of a moral individual who takes a stand against oppression in a specific historical context.

The novel, composed largely of the judge's thoughts and conversations as filtered through the narrator, relies heavily upon a particularly literate and orderly form of stream of consciousness. The character of the judge is gradually revealed to the reader through insights provided by the narrator into the judge's train of thought. In an interior monologue capturing the protagonist's reflections as he leaves the Palazzo di Giustizia, the judge contemplates the irony of justice being dispensed from the very edifice that had served as the seat of the Inquisition. This is an irony that defines for Sciascia *la sicilianità* and one upon which he has commented at some length. The judge's meditation upon the fanaticism and cruelty of the Inquisition at this particular juncture is intimately linked to his emotions surrounding the pending trial and his rejection of the expected sentence of death. The judge articulates his opposition to the death penalty by borrowing from Montaigne's comment on the execution of Martin Guerre: 'Dopotutto, significa dare un bel peso alle proprie opinioni, se per esse si fa arrostire vivo un uomo' (*Opere,* 3:339–40) [When all's said and done, it attaches tremendous weight to one's own opinions if a man is roasted alive for their sake]

(*Open Doors,* 19).[5] By following the character's train of thought, the reader is reminded of the intimate link between past and present. There is a link not only between the Inquisition of the fifteenth century and fascist Italy of the 1930s, but also between the events of 1937 recounted in the novel and the 'present' moment from which the novel has been written. The fact that the clock has been turned back, that the events of the novel are being recounted not only with hindsight but from a specific moment in 'present'-day Italy, is underscored as the narrator follows the character's train of thought from the Inquisition to the present: 'non si può fare arrostire vivo un uomo soltanto perché certe opinioni non condivide. E tranne quella, qui, oggi, anno 1937 (anno 1987) che l'umanità, il diritto, la legge ... rispondere con l'assassinio all'assassinio non debbano' *(Opere,* 3:340) [you cannot roast a man alive because he does not share certain opinions. And except the opinion, here and now in 1937 (1987) that humanity, justice, law ... must not answer murder with murder] (*Open Doors,* 19). The interior monologue of the character is disrupted by the contemporary author's reference to the 'present' moment of writing. This moment of rupture underscores the intimate link between past and present.

The ethical foundation on which the judge's opposition to the death penalty is based is constructed from a wealth of literary sources. The narrator gives the reader insight into the judge's train of thought as he meditates on literary denunciations of the death penalty, from Montaigne's denunciation of the Martin Guerre sentence to more recent treatments of the subject. An excerpt from Brancati lays bare the misfortune of the poor man who not only suffers from iniquity but can find no words to express his suffering. Neither a verse of Milton nor of Leopardi comes to the aid of the uneducated man, who cannot articulate why he suffers. The narrator contrasts the poor man's lack of literary inspiration to the wealth of literary sources at the judge's disposal. Although the narrator does not name his source, the words of Tolstoy come first to the judge's mind. In *A Confession,* Tolstoy's account of his ethical and spiritual crisis and his growing discontent with civil society, the author describes his reaction as he witnesses an execution. These words are indelibly traced in the judge's memory: 'Quando vidi come la testa si staccava dal corpo e come l'una e l'altro, separatamente, andavano a sbattere nella cassa, allora capii ... che non vi è alcuna teoria della razionalità dell'esistente e del progresso che possa giustificare un simile atto' *(Opere,* 3:340) [When I saw how the head split away from the body, and how each landed separately in the crate, then I realized ... that there is no theory of the rationality of life or of progress that can justify such an act] (*Open Doors*, 19). It is clear that this work has occupied a cherished place on the judge's bookshelf, as the narrator refers to the translation of Tolstoy's *A Confession* received by the judge as a boy in the winter of 1913. But it is to another unnamed Russian writer that the judge awards the highest praise for his denunciation of the death penalty. In a reference to Dostoievsky's 1868 *The Idiot*, the judge recalls the page on the death penalty: 'il principe ... racconta di un'esecuzione capitale cui ha assistito ... e svolge contro la pena di morte il più alto discorso che mai si sia stato fatto' (*Opere*, 3:341) [the Prince ... is telling of an execution he has witnessed ... and ... pours out the most inspired attack on capital punishment that has ever been made] (*Open Doors*, 20). Sciascia himself was particularly struck by Dostoievsky's indictment of the death penalty, and quoted the relevant passage from *The Idiot* in its entirety in his diary, *Nero su nero*.[6] The judge's tributes to Montaigne, Dostoievsky, Tolstoy, and Brancati mark the beginning of a process that will continue throughout the novel. The narrator assiduously gives the reader insight into the judge's character by revealing the texts that occupy his leisure hours and inform his ethical choices.

The judge musters his arguments against the death penalty throughout the course of the trial. As the trial proceeds, the evidence against the accused becomes more and more damning. Yet despite the atrocity of the crime and the accused's unrepentant admission of guilt, the judge continues to indulge in meditations that will strengthen his resolve to resist the expected outcome: 'Così meditando ... ricollegandone certi momenti alla memoria di cose lette e cose lette pensate, il piccolo giudice si avvicinava all'imputato e alla sua contorta e feroce umanità, alla sua follia' (*Opere*, 3:363) [And so, thinking over the technicalities of the trial and linking certain moments in it with things he had read, or thought about things he had read, the little judge drew imperceptibly closer to the defendant, to his fierce, twisted humanity, to his madness] (*Open Doors*, 42). The judge is fully convinced of the guilt of the accused. Yet he also holds a strong conviction of the accused's humanity. The latter is based upon the judge's ability to *see* the other. His opposition to the death penalty rests upon an ethic that is remarkably similar to that of Emmanuel Levinas. Waldenfels has analyzed Levinas's idea that the relation to the other (*l'autrui*) that lies at the basis of any ethical system is a corporeal, 'face to face' relation that cannot be reduced to comprehension: 'The "face" is no mere metaphor transporting a figurative sense into a higher sphere, delivering it from its corporeal chains. Levinas' ethics are rooted in a phenomenology of the body ... It is the hungering, thirsting, enjoying, suffering, working, loving, murdering human being in all its corporeality [*Leibhaftigkeit*] whose otherness is at stake' (65).[7] The judge's interior monologue harks back to Levinas's insistence on the humanity of the other, even the murdering other, a humanity based on the corporeality of the *autrui*. The judge does not so much comprehend the accused as see him in all his 'contorta e feroce umanità.' The use of the phrase 'as was his duty' to describe the judge's relation to the other is an acknowledgment of the ethical responsibility to the other human being, 'that being to whom I am obliged before being comprehended' (Critchley and Bernasconi, 10).

It is important to note that the judge does not frame his opposition to the death penalty in political terms. As the narrator points out, the judge has an aversion to fascism but refuses to consider himself anti-fascist: 'rifiutava di considerarsi anti-fascista, al fascismo soltanto opponendo la sua dignità nel pensare e nell'agire' (*Opere*, 3:363) [he refused to consider himself an anti-fascist, merely opposing to fascism his personal dignity in thought and action] (*Open Doors*, 42). This disclaimer underscores the fact that the judge acts out of ethical and not political conviction.[8] Towards the close of the trial, the judge goes home and begins to leaf through the *ricordi* of a sixteenth-century Palermitan writer, Argisto Giuffredi. Addressed to a son who was preparing for a career in the law, the memoir, entitled *Avvertimenti cristiani*, admonishes the son not to resort to torture ('la frusta') or the death penalty 'per qualsivoglia cosa: '"So bene" diceva il Giuffredi "che questo vi parrà un riguardo stravagante": e altro che, se poteva parere: due secoli prima del Beccaria. E come era arrivato, il Giuffredi, a quell'idea "stravagante"?' (*Opere*, 3:368) ['I know full well,' said Giuffredi, 'that this will seem to you an extravagant opinion'; and it certainly must have seemed so, two centuries before Beccaria. How had Giuffredi arrived at that 'extravagant' idea?] (*Open Doors*, 47). The reference to Cesare Beccaria, the eighteenth century Milanese author of *Dei delitti e delle pene*, reminds the reader of that writer's passionate indictment of torture and the death penalty.[9] Yet it is significant that Sciascia filters the judge's opposition to the death penalty not through the lens of Cesare Beccaria, but rather through Giuffredi. Sciascia devotes many pages of the novel to this relatively obscure Palermitan writer, whose *ricordi* were discovered in a manuscript in the nineteenth century. While the judge admires Beccaria's *Dei delitti e delle pene*, he is struck by the prescience of a writer who, two centuries before Beccaria and the Italian Enlightenment, in a century given over to the excesses of the Inquisition, showed remarkable insight into the pernicious effects of torture and capital punishment on society. As the judge sets down his copy of Giuffredi's memoir, the narrator remarks:

> Amava molto sgomitolare tra i suoi libri e nei suoi pensieri, il filo di estemporanee curiosità. Da quando aveva cominciato ad avere a che fare coi libri, e perciò i suoi fratelli, che sui libri stavano con più volontà e fatica, lo consideravano un perdigiorno. Ma sapeva di aver tanto guadagnato ... (*Opere*, 3:369)

> [He had always loved to unravel a thread of spontaneous curiosity through his books and in his thoughts, ever since he had had dealings with books; which was why his brothers, whose relations with books required will power and effort, thought him a time-waster. But he knew how much he had gained from those wasted hours and days.] (*Open Doors*, 48)

The judge's musings reinforce the idea of reading as a necessary and fruitful nourishment of the mind and not a waste of time.

The ninth scene of the novel opens with a reflection on the exclusion of Giuffredi from the 'canon' of great Sicilian writers, as defined by the fascist regime. This is followed by a scene in the anteroom of the courtroom in which the judge, donning his robe, asks the most sympathetic juror, the *agricoltore*, whether he is familiar with Giuffredi's work. When the juror, much to the judge's surprise, responds in the affirmative, the judge adds the detail that he has been rereading Giuffredi. The juror nods in agreement, as if approving of the judge's reading. This complicity between the judge and the juror is established through the simple exchange of authors and titles. Indeed, as the narrator points out: 'Il nome di uno scrittore, il titolo di un libro, possono a volte, per alcuni, suonare come quello di una patria' (*Opere*, 3:366) [Sometimes, for some people, the name of a writer, the title of a book, can ring out like the name of one's homeland] (*Open Doors*, 45).

Porte aperte is the portrait of a principled man whose ethical framework is shaped and defined by his reading. The shared recognition of the power of Giuffredi's work and the force of his argument is the first instalment in the defence of the power of the pen in Sciascia's penultimate novel. By acknowledging their appreciation for the work of an early opponent of capital punishment, an 'enlightened' writer whose work preceded the Enlightenment by two centuries, the judge and juror not only establish their shared conviction of the sanctity of human life. They also establish the importance of reading in shaping the ethical framework within which they make this judgment. It is significant that the power of the pen moves not only the protagonist, *il piccolo giudice*, but also the juror and his French ladyfriend. These kindred spirits, who casually exchange references to the works of Montaigne, Zweig, Brancati, Tolstoy, Dostoievkski, Giuffredi, Beccaria, Guicciardini, Verga, Stendhal, Della Porta, and Pitré, share in the judge's passion for reading and his conviction of its moral efficacy.

The narrator of *Porte aperte* gradually reveals himself to be another kindred spirit, a reading man whose admiration for the judge matches the juror's. The narrator evolves over the course of the novel. At first, he functions as a disembodied, omniscient voice, providing the reader access to the judge's innermost thoughts. Gradually, however, he reveals himself to be a character in his own right. This begins to become apparent in such passages as the opening paragraph of chapter 9, after the episode in which the judge has been rereading and meditating upon Giuffredi's memoir. The subsequent scene begins with the bemused observation that, in all the celebrations of illustrious Sicilians sponsored by the fascist regime, none had ever recognized the grandeur of Giuffredi and his denunciation of torture and capital punishment. The exact circumstances of the discovery of this precious *ricordo* are reported with a reflection on the relevance of the document in the historical context of the year in which it was discovered (1896). The subsequent paragraph begins 'Ma tornando al giudice' (*Opere*, 3:371) [But to return to the judge] (*Open Doors*, 50.) It is at this moment that the reader notes a kind of slippage. The stream of consciousness with which the scene opens reflects the thought process not of the judge but of the dramatized narrator, who has passed from filtering the character's thoughts on the significance of Giuffredi's eloquent work to adding his own.[10] The judge's appreciation of Giuffredi's heroic and almost anachronistic *ricordo* is shared not only by his new-found friend, the juror, but also by the admiring narrator. The narrator, that is, shares in the growing complicity between the judge and the juror. The slippage in the stream of consciousness between the character and the narrator underscores the continuity between the two. The narrator has tremendous admiration for the judge and for the value of his story. As we shall discuss shortly, in the penultimate scene the reader learns that the narrator had met the judge some years after the events recorded in the novel.

The trial proceeds in a predictable fashion. As we have noted, there is no doubt of the accused's guilt. Each of the crimes was premeditated and brutal. The accused admitted to having invited his wife on an outing to visit their grown children on which he would proceed to stab her to death, after encouraging her first to pray for eternal salvation. After the murder of his wife he went first to the home of the accountant and then to the home of avvocato Bruno, using on each the same bloodstained dagger with which he had taken his wife's life. The innumerable lies of the accused only serve further to condemn him. The defence rests and the deliberations begin. The brutality of the crime and the premeditation not only merit a guilty verdict: they also may be exploited to justify a sentence of death. Yet despite the incontrovertible evidence of guilt, after a short discussion the court emerges from chambers with a sentence other than death. Both the judge and the jurors have remained true to their principles.

The end of the novel does not coincide with the conclusion of the trial. It is clear that the case is not closed; the sentence will be overturned by a higher court and the death penalty will ultimately be imposed on the accused by the fascist regime. The narrator's attention, however, focuses not on the legal arena but on the judge's encounters in the aftermath of the trial. The judge had scrupulously denied himself the luxury of fully enjoying the juror's friendship until after the trial's conclusion. In the penultimate scene of *Porte aperte* the judge is able to satisfy his curiosity about this well-read and moral farmer when he pays him a visit at his country house. As the juror explains, his library, along with the house and lands, had been purchased by his illiterate grandfather from an impoverished noble family. The story of the juror's family undone by its debts is glossed by the judge through references to Guicciardini and Verga, authors well known to the juror. The judge's enjoyment of the friendship with the highly literate juror is laid bare: 'Aveva una sete di parlare di libri, di scrittori: tanto raramente gli capitava di imbattersi in persone con cui potesse' (*Opere*, 3:391) [He felt a sort of thirst to talk about books and writers, so rarely did he come across people with whom he could do so] (*Open Doors*, 69). The literary colloquy continues and is joined by the juror's ladyfriend, a French woman and Stendhalian Italophile who has come to appreciate Italy through the written word. The juror's wry observation on the *francese italianizzante* is, 'Amava di noi quello che noi, di noi stessi, detestiamo' (*Opere*, 3:393) [They love what we most detest in ourselves] (*Open Doors*, 70).[11] At first glance, the entire leisurely conversation might seem to be a digression, a literary interlude that has little bearing on the plot. Yet in many ways the interlude underscores one of the most significant facets of the judge's character, and of Sciascia's novel. The conviction of the weight of the written word in the ethical formation of the individual and the moral resolve to be drawn from sharing one's reading with others are the characteristic features of the protagonist of Sciascia's *Porte aperte*.

Here Sciascia builds upon a theme that he initially touched upon in his first and defining book, *Le parrocchie di Regalpetra* (1956).[12] In 'Breve cronaca del regime' he paints a portrait of Racalmuto, a fictionalized version of the author's birthplace of Regalpetra during the fascist period. One of the most significant subplots of *Le parrocchie di Regalpetra* is the story of the author's gradual conversion to anti-fascism and the pivotal role played by reading books and frequenting the company of fellow readers. Growing up in a family in which his father believed in Mussolini but not in fascism, and his aunt, a surrogate mother, kept a picture of the anti-fascist martyr Giacomo Matteotti in her sewing basket, Sciascia, like other youth of the period, was at first caught up in the enthusiasm of the early years of the fascist regime. As he grew into adolescence, the author began to see that regime through a different lens. As he records in *Le parrocchie di Regalpetra*, the young Sciascia met a professor 'che mi aveva intelligentemente guidato nelle letture' (*Opere*, 1:42) [who had intelligently guided me in my readings] (*Salt in the Wound*, 34).[13] He began to read Dos Passos and other American authors of the period, and frequented the church-sponsored *letture dantesche*, whose subversive 'letture cariche di intenzioni segrete' [readings loaded with hidden intentions] (*Opere*, 1:43) began to attract the attention of the fascist authorities. And, as the author concludes this brief chronicle, his exposure to the right books during his formative years was pivotal: 'mi trovai dunque dall'altra parte' (*Opere*, 1:43) [I found myself on the other side]. As told by Sciascia, his conversion to antifascism was not a result of the solitary pursuit of reading. The emphasis is on the reading of books as a community activity, on discussion and on interaction with other readers, either his peers, as in the case of the *letture dantesche*, or his mentor, the professor. This same depiction of reading as a civic activity, not a solitary pastime, is also very much in evidence in *Porte aperte*.

The narrator implicitly engages the reader in the activity of discussing and evaluating books throughout the novel. The text functions as a primer, an annotated bibliography of ethically informed writers. The excerpts liberally interspersed throughout the novel give the reader an introduction to important writers and works to add to his or her bookshelf. Occasionally, the narrator explicitly involves the reader in the exercise of judgment informed by reading, as in the conclusion to the eighth chapter: 'noi lasciamo che ogni lettore cherchi da sé le risposte' (*Opere*, 3:369) [we leave it to each reader to seek his own answers] (*Open Doors*, 49). The reader, it is implied, may become another kindred spirit who draws upon shared readings for ethical nourishment.

The judge's visit to the juror is prefaced by an anecdote that contributes further to the portrait of the dramatized narrator and his relationship to the protagonist. The narrator finally explains why he has referred to the judge throughout the novel as *il piccolo giudice*. When the judge was first pointed out to the narrator, he happened to be the smallest in stature in a group of others.

> Aveva una brillante carriera da fare, se l'è rovinata rifiutando di condannare uno a morte'; e mi raccontò sommariamente e con qualche imprecisione la storia di quel processo. Da quel momento, ogni volta che poi l'ho visto, e nelle poche volte in cui gli ho parlato, il dirlo piccolo mi è parso ne misurasse la grandezza: per le cose tanto più forti di lui che aveva serenamente affrontato. (*Opere*, 3:389)

> He had a brilliant career ahead of him, but he ruined it by refusing to condemn a man to death, and he gave me a rather sketchy account of the trial. From then on, every time I saw him, and on the few occasions when I spoke to him, it seemed a measure of his greatness to call him small: because of the things so much more powerful than himself that he had confronted with serenity. (*Open Doors*, 67)

This reference to the several encounters the narrator had with the judge over the years, as well as the few precious occasions he had to speak with him, serves to confirm the status of the narrator as a *dramatis persona* in his own right. He is not a disembodied narrator, but rather a participant observer. A younger man than the judge, the narrator had admired the judge as a man whose 'grandezza' had nothing to do with physical stature. The indication that the judge's story was originally recounted to the narrator with some inaccuracies ('qualche imprecisione') shows the reader that the latter has gone to the trouble to discover the truth about the judge, to get his story right.

The encounter between the juror and the judge confirms the narrator's assessment of the judge's moral stature. The juror greets his visitor with words of praise for his courage during the course of the trial: 'L'ho ammirato molto, in camera di consiglio: lei è riuscito a porre il problema della pena di morte, nei suoi termini più angosciosi senza mai riferirsi direttamente' (*Opere*, 3:395) [I felt a great admiration for you in the council chamber: you managed to pose the problem of the death penalty in the most terrible terms without ever referring to it directly]' (*Open Doors*, 73). The juror then confides in the judge that he, too, welcomed the assignment, which allowed him to make a gesture against the death penalty. The scene concludes as judge and juror agree that, while each man's position against the death penalty may constitute the point of honour of their lives, their gestures may ultimately prove to be futile.

The final chapter of *Porte aperte*, however, belies this pessimistic prediction. When the prosecutor calls the judge into his office three months after the conclusion of the triple murder trial, both are agreed that the judge's career is, indeed, in ruins. Neither is surprised by this outcome. The prosecutor asks the judge whether the jury, in rejecting the death penalty, did not simply surrender to the judge's opinion. The latter insists that this was not the case, that the jury was not merely expressing an opinion but holding firm to a principle. The judge continues: 'Ed è un principio di tale forza, quello contro la pena di morte, che si può essere certi di essere nel giusto anche se si resti soli a sostenerlo' (*Opere*, 3:397) [And the principle of opposition to capital punishment is so strong that you can feel quite sure you're in the right, even if you're alone in maintaining it] (*Open Doors*, 75). The force of this principle is confirmed in the conclusion of *Porte aperte*, in which the prosecutor confesses to the judge his own change of heart: 'Ma mi ci sto adattando: sto cominciando a pensare cose cui finora non ho pensato. E per esempio: che sono stato un morto che ha seppellito altri morti' (*Opere*, 3:398) [But I'm adapting; I'm starting to think things I haven't thought till now. For example: that I have been a dead man who has buried other dead men] (*Open Doors*, 76). The moral example set by the judge has not been futile. Although the judge's sentence will unquestionably be reversed by a higher court and the accused will ultimately receive the death penalty, the principle of the obligation of the state to protect the sanctity of human life has been defended. The judge allows himself to consider for a moment the possibility that others might follow his example: 'Io ho salvato la mia anima, i giurati hanno salvato la loro: il che può anche apparire molto comodo. Ma pensi se avvenisse, in concatenazione, che ogni giudice badasse a salvare la propria' (*Opere*, 3:400–1) [I saved my soul, the jurors have saved theirs, which may all sound very convenient. But just think if every judge, one after another, were concerned to save his] (*Open Doors*, 79). The final chapter of the novel, focusing as it does on the way in which the judge with his courageous stand against capital punishment has made the prosecutor uneasy in his former convictions, holds out a glimmer of hope. There is hope, that is, that the acceptance of the status quo can be disturbed. The prosecutor, who in the first chapter of the novel reminds the judge, 'Lei sa come la penso' [You know my thinking] and who warns his colleague not to take a stand against the status quo, is in a state of unawareness. The pronoun 'la' in the expression 'come la penso' refers to a host of received ideas that have held humankind hostage and blocked the exercise of reason. As the narrator of *Porte aperte* observes: '"la" ... la cosa cui non si vuole parlare ... Pronome, per gli italiani, della religione cattolica, del partito al governo, della massoneria, di ogni cosa che avesse ... forza e potere ... e ora del fascismo' (*Opere*, 3:330) [the thing ... the thing you don't want to name ... A phrase that, for Italians, belonged to the Catholic religion, the governing party, Freemasonry, anything that had – obviously or, worse, obscurely – force and power ... and now belonged to fascism] (*Open Doors*, 8). It is Sciascia's hope that society can progress from acceptance of the status quo as reflected in 'come la penso' to a more rigorous and rational 'come penso.' Sciascia implicitly exhorts his reader to exercise the power of reason captured in the verb *penso*.

Porte aperte ends with the protagonist's beguiling fantasy of a world that recognizes and honours the sanctity of human life. In a variation on Calderon's metaphor, *la vida es sueno*, the judge presents his utopian vision of the world:

> Se tutto questo, il mondo, la vita, noi stessi, altro non è, come è stato detto, che il sogno di qualcuno, questo dettaglio infinitesimo del suo sogno, questo caso di cui stiamo a discutere, l'agonia del condannato, la mia, la sua, può anche servire ad avvertirlo che sta sognando male, che si volti su altro fianco, che cerchi di avere sogni migliori. (*Opere*, 3:401)

> [If all this – the world, life, ourselves – is nothing but someone's dream, as

has been said, then this infinitesimal detail in his dream, the case we're discussing, the condemned man's agony, mine, yours, may yet serve to alert the dreamer that he is having nightmares, that he should turn over and try to have better dreams.] (*Open Doors*, 79)

Whether he is focusing on the injustice of the fascist regime and its re-establishment of the death penalty, the injustices of 1980s Italy, or the injustice of the present day, it is Sciascia's hope that the novel can play a part in awakening the reader from his or her nightmare to a vision of a better world.

2 The Death of the Detective in *Il Cavaliere e la morte*

Like the novels of the sixties and early seventies that established Leonardo Sciascia's literary reputation – *Il giorno della civetta*, *A ciascuno il suo*, *Il contesto*, and *Todo modo* – his penultimate novel, *Il cavaliere e la morte* (1988), takes the familiar form of the *giallo*. The detective genre is a mode of discourse grounded in an implicit faith in the power of reason. The affront to reason is the point of departure of the conventional detective novel, and the satisfaction of reason is its conclusion.[1] It has been suggested that the detective story as a *forma mentis* belongs to the Enlightenment, a period to which Sciascia repeatedly turned for inspiration.[2] Sciascia often identified himself as an 'enlightened' man.[3] In the introduction to his inaugural work, *Le parrocchie di Regalpetra*, he resoundingly declares: 'Credo nella ragione umana, e nella libertà e nella giustizia che dalla ragione scaturiscono' (9) [I believe in human reason, and in the liberty and justice it engenders] (*Salt in the Wound*, v). Yet despite this credo, Sciascia's detective novels do not present the detective as the embodiment of the triumph of reason; his fictional heroes are inevitably defeated.[4] Moreover, his detective novels invariably deal with unjust, corrupt societies – the antithesis of the 'mondo illuminato dalla ragione' in which the classical *giallo* is set. In *Il cavaliere e la morte* Sciascia adopts many of the conventions of the detective genre. The author's familiarity with these norms is evident not only throughout his fiction but also in such critical essays as 'Breve storia del romanzo poliziesco.' Sciascia uses his mastery of the rules of the game not to satisfy the reader's expectations of order and closure, but more often to thwart the expectations awakened by his generic choice. Like Dacia Maraini and Antonio Tabucchi, he exploits the genre in order to expose injustice and pass judgment on the guilty party.

Il cavaliere e la morte is set in a country that can be loosely identified as Italy but that lacks the kind of 'local colour' and quasi-anthropological detail characterizing Sciascia's first two novels, *Il giorno della civetta* and *A ciascuno il suo*. The crime investigated in *Il cavaliere e la morte* is not linked to a specifically Sicilian or Italian sociopolitical context. The author used his earlier detective fiction first to expose the pervasiveness of the Sicilian mafia and then to expose the larger mafia of power in Rome. In *Il cavaliere e la morte*, however, Sciascia's target is both larger and less well defined. As the author himself observed, there is a marked progression in his writing, in which the focus shifts away from the problems of his native land and towards more universal and intractable ills. In his 1979 *La Sicilia come metafora*, Sciascia comments:

> C'è stato un progressivo superamento dei miei orizzonti, e poco alla volta non mi sono più sentito siciliano, o meglio, non più solamente siciliano ... la Sicilia offre la rappresentazione di tanti problemi, di tante contraddizioni ... anche europei, al punto di costituire la metafora del mondo odierno. (78)

> [There has been a progressive widening of my horizons and little by little I have no longer felt Sicilian, or better, not only Sicilian ... Sicily offers the representation of so many problems, of so many contradictions ... even European ones, so that it comes to constitute a metaphor of our world.]

The target in *Il cavaliere e la morte* (represented by the figure of the devil in the Dürer engraving) may be said to be the corruption of power itself. The magnitude of that evil is of a greater dimension than in Sciascia's first detective novels, in which the defeat of justice is situated in either a Sicilian or an Italian context.[5] In *Il cavaliere e la morte*, on the contrary, the protagonist suffers not only for a particular time, place, or people but for what Elio Vittorini in *Conversazione in Sicilia* calls 'i mali del mondo offeso' [the ills of the offended world]. The impending death of the protagonist of *Il cavaliere e la morte*, and of the author, makes the problem of the corruption of power more urgent and the injustice more intolerable than in any of Sciascia's previous works.

Il cavaliere e la morte features a protagonist who bears no small resemblance to the author himself. The novel was written shortly before Sciascia's death from cancer in 1989. Like Tolstoy's *The Death of Ivan Illich*, a novel to which Sciascia's protagonist refers on more than one occasion, *Il cavaliere e la morte* concerns the thoughts on life and death of a dying man. The questions that the fictional character ponders are akin to those that the author himself is pondering in his dying days. *Il cavaliere e la morte* opens as the deputy of an unnamed police force is contemplating on his office wall the sixteenth-century Dürer engraving *The Knight, Death and the Devil*. The novel not only tells the story of the deputy's last case. As the title suggests, Sciascia's text is a meditation on injustice and evil and on the need for a 'knight' to combat injustice in the world. Like the various investigator/protagonists in Sciascia's novels, from Captain Bellodi of *Il giorno della civetta* to Professor Laurana of *A ciascuno il suo*, the 'knight' symbolized in the Dürer engraving represents the moral individual at battle in a flawed or immoral world.

The deputy's last case centres on the shadowy mafia of power that knows no national or historical boundaries. Two detectives, known only as the chief and the deputy, are beginning an investigation into the murder of the influential lawyer Sandoz. The chief is a northern Italian while the protagonist, the deputy, is an expatriate, a Sicilian living in a large Italian city where 'southerners' are looked down upon. On the body of the murder victim a placecard has been recovered bearing the name Cesare Aurispa and the words 'I'll kill you.' The deputy and his superior call upon Aurispa, the powerful president of United Industries, to question him about the incriminating card. In deference to the president's position, the chief guarantees him impunity from the outset of the investigation: 'Siamo venuti a infastidirla ... per chiederle qualcosa che può non significar nulla, come può essere invece un punto di partenza per le indagini, indagini, beninteso, che comunque non toccherebbero lei' (*Opere*, 3:413) [We had to come and disturb you ... to ask you something that might be entirely meaningless, but could just as easily provide the starting point for our investigations: investigations which, I need hardly say, will not affect you, your person] (*The Knight and Death*, 7).[6] The president offers an apparently plausible explanation for the note on the placecard. He explains that the threat jotted on the card was part of a standing joke between himself and his friend, Sandoz. At a dinner organized by the local cultural society Sandoz had been seated next to an attractive woman, Signora De Matis. Aurispa claims that he was simply feigning jealousy of Sandoz's flirtation with her when he wrote the 'playful' death threat. When asked by the police whether he can suggest any other lines of inquiry to be pursued, the president casually offers one. Sandoz had allegedly confided to the president shortly before his death that he had received a threatening phone call from a revolutionary group calling themselves the Children of '89. While Sandoz did not take the group or the threat seriously, the president now invites the authorities to follow this lead.

The lines of inquiry of the two investigators differ sharply. The deputy insists upon pursuing the trail leading to the president as the culprit. The chief is inclined to follow the lead provided by the president, towards the terrorist group Children of '89. The latter confirms the president's story, that Sandoz had indeed received phone calls from a group calling themselves the Children of '89 and that the victim had dismissed their death threats as a joke. Is the revolutionary group Children of '89 responsible for the crime? Or is this solution too simple? The nature of the alleged terrorist group and the meaning of their name, Children of '89, are debated by the deputy and his superior. The chief interprets it as a reference to the 'present' year of 1989, while the deputy speculates that the name is a reference to 1789, the year in which the revolution was born. The chief fondly disagrees and admonishes the deputy for his obsession with history. This is an admonition that could be directed at Sciascia himself. Indeed, this exchange represents another of a score of clues identifying the protagonist as an authorial surrogate. The deputy, more than Bellodi, Laurana, or Rogas, the investigators in Sciascia's earlier detective novels, is unabashedly presented as a mirror image of the author himself. The deputy dismisses the Children of '89 as a 'red-herring' and pursues the more promising and obvious line of inquiry leading towards the president as the guilty party.

The deputy is an 'old-school' detective in the tradition of classical detective fiction. Sciascia patterns his character on the archetype of the detective as outlined in 'Breve storia del romanzo poliziesco':

> L'incoruttibilità e infallibilità dell'investigatore, la sua quasi ascetica vita (generalmente non ha famiglia, non ha ambizioni, non ha beni, ha una certa inclinazione alla misoginia e alla misantropia, ...), le sue capacità di leggere il delitto nel cuore umano oltre che nelle cose ... lo investono di luce metafisica, ne fanno un eletto. (*Opere*, 2:1183)

> [The incorruptibility and infallibility of the investigator, his almost ascetic life (generally he has no family, no ambitions, no goods, and a certain tendency towards misogyny and misanthropy ...) his ability to read crime in the human heart more than in objects ... bathe him in a metaphysical light, make him a chosen one.

The deputy is the embodiment of astuteness, dedication to duty, and integrity. He considers no one to be above suspicion. He insists on verifying the president's story, particularly his claim to have disposed of Sandoz's response to his 'playful' death threat. The chief, recognizing the president as 'untouchable,' tries to steer the deputy away from the president as prime suspect: 'un'indagine in questo senso il Presidente la prenderebble in malaparte' (*Opere*, 3:419) [any investigation in this direction would hardly be viewed in a kindly light by the President] (*Knight*, 11). The deputy nonetheless pursues his line of inquiry with dogged dedication to ferreting out the truth. While the chief is busy constructing the official story, which will implicate the Children of '89 and exonerate the president, he nonetheless allows the protagonist to work in the opposite direction. He gives the deputy two men to assist in an all-night search through the garbage in which the president claims to have discarded Sandoz's response. The response is nowhere to be found. The chapter concludes, 'L'immondizia non mente mai' (*Opere*, 3:421) [Garbage never lies (*The Knight*, 12) casting doubt on the line of inquiry suggested by the president and on his nonchalant cover story characterizing the death threat as a joke.

In the classical *giallo* the key to the mystery emerges slowly over the course of the novel. Any solution to the crime that takes shape in the early pages of the novel often proves to be a false solution, a dead end. In Sciascia's *Il cavaliere e la morte;* the reader follows the deputy's lead to the identification of the most likely suspect in chapter 3. The deputy's theory, that the president is indeed guilty and that he is somehow involved in the creation of the Children of '89 as a smokescreen concealing a wide network of illegal activity, proves to be correct: 'Questa associazione non esiste, ma la si vuole fare esistere: schermo e spettro di tutt'altre intenzioni' (*Opere*, 3:423) [This association does not exist, but somebody wants to will it into existence, as a shield and a spectre for quite different purposes] (*Knight*, 14). The chief half-heartedly disagrees and accuses the deputy of an overactive imagination fueled by his reading of detective novels: 'la sua è una linea romanzesca, da romanzo poliziesco diciamo classico, di quelli che i lettori, ormai smaliziati, arrivano a indovinare come va a finire dopo aver letto le prime venti pagine' (*Opere*, 3:424) [the line you are following is lifted straight from fiction, from one of those books they call a classical detective novel, where the sharp-witted reader can guess, after the first twenty pages, how it is all going to turn out] (*Knight* 15). This meta-narrative comment on the norms of the genre that Sciascia is exploiting in the novel draws the reader into the game of detection. Is it true that the reader of the classical detective novel solves the crime in the first twenty-five pages? Sciascia himself dismisses this notion of the reader's relationship to the genre in his 'Breve storia del romanzo poliziesco.' Rather than perpetuate the idea that the reader tries to match wits with the detective, Sciascia instead focuses on the way in which the reader avoids at all costs a premature solution of the mystery and relaxes into a state of intellectual repose. In any case, the reader of *Il cavaliere e la morte* is alerted to the likelihood of a premature solution to the puzzle by the chief's ineffectual protestations. Indeed, the sharp-witted reader does conclude that the deputy's conviction is correct, that the president of United Industries is in fact the author of the crime.

The question remaining to be answered midway through Sciascia's *giallo* is not 'whodunnit,' but why. While there is no doubt that the president and his associates have created the Children of '89, the question of motive remains. The deputy must discover whether the Children of '89 were created to murder Sandoz, or whether Sandoz was murdered in order to create a scapegoat, the Children of '89. The detective fills in this piece of the puzzle when he visits his friend Rieti, an operative in the secret intelligence service of the country. Rieti provides the motive for the crime and confirms the deputy's suspicion of the president's guilt. Sandoz had become aware of large-scale corruption by the president and had threatened to expose him. The deputy and Rieti speculate that, beyond this personal vendetta, there is a larger motive underlying the crime. 'They,' the shadowy associates of the president, needed a victim in order to create the Children of '89. 'Si può sospettare, dunque, che esista una segreta carta costituzionale che al primo articolo reciti: la sicurezza del potere si fonda sull'insicurezza dei cittadini' (*Opere*, 3:442) [There are grounds for suspecting, in other words, that there is in existence a secret constitution whose first article runs: The security of power is based on the insecurity of the citizens] (*Knight*, 32). A revolutionary group was needed to consolidate the power of the president and of United Industries. The murder of Sandoz was primarily a convenient means to that end.

It has been suggested that the detective novel appeals to the reader inasmuch as it dramatizes 'the spectacle of the human mind at work.'[6] The satisfaction derived from that spectacle begins to wane for the reader of *Il cavaliere e la morte* as the novel progresses. If the culprit is identified in chapter 3 and the motive of the crime is uncovered midway through the novel, what remains to be discovered in this unconventional detective novel?[7] The question that holds the attention of the reader until the final pages of *Il cavaliere e la morte* is, What will become of the investigator who has identified the guilty party but is powerless to bring him to justice? As early as chapter 5, when the deputy pays his visit to Signora De Matis, Sandoz's dinner comanion on the night of his murder, she observes that the futility of the investigation weighs upon the deputy. She comments: 'Se lei mi risponde che non si può molto, credo si possa arguire che non si può nulla. E lei mi pare che ne soffra' (*Opere*, 3:431) [If you tell me there is not a great deal to be done, I think it can be deduced that there is nothing to be done. The thing is that you appear to suffer over that] (*Knight*, 22). When the deputy rejoins that he suffers over so many things, Signora De Matis draws upon D.H. Lawrence's reading of Verga's *Mastro-Don Gesualdo* to locate the roots of the deputy's state of mind in his Sicilian origins. Just as Sicily in Sciascia's later works becomes a metaphor of the flawed 'mondo odierno,' so 'la sicilianità' comes to signify that profound sense of pessimism that characterizes the deputy.[8] The deputy does not disagree with the erudite De Matis's diagnosis of his *sicilianità*.[9] Instead he ends the visit by steering the conversation towards reading and rereading. 'Lei legge molto, vero? ... Io ... trovo ormai più gusto nel rileggere: si scoprono cose che alla prima lettura non c'erano ... e sa che cosa sto rileggendo? *Le anime morte*: pieno di cose che non c'erano' (*Opere*, 3:432–3) [You read a lot, don't you? I ... find more enjoyment in rereading: you discover things which were not there at the first reading ... I mean, were not there for me ... Do you know what I am rereading? *Dead Souls*: packed full of things which were not there before] (*Knight*, 23). The deputy's defence of rereading in the encounter with Signora De Matis provides a valuable key to his character.

The protagonist of *Il cavaliere e la morte*, like the judge in Sciascia's *Porte aperte*, is above all distinguished as a voracious reader. The characters who people the pages of the deputy's favourite books become his constant companions. He identifies his office in Rome as adjacent to the office of don Ciccio Ingravallo, the detective protagonist of Gadda's open-ended detective novel *Quer pasticciaccio brutto de Via Merulana*: 'poiché gli pareva, tanta era la verità delle pagine di Gadda, di averlo conosciuto in quegli uffici e non in quelle pagine' (*Opere*, 3:455) [because such was the truth of the pages of Gadda's novel that he had the impression of having bumped into him in those offices rather than on the printed page] (*Knight*, 44–5). Many of the writers on his bookshelf – Hugo, Montaigne, Leopardi, Verga, Stevenson,

Gadda, Tolstoy, Gide, Borges, Gogol – are the same writers whose works fill the library of the 'little judge' of *Porte aperte*. Authors whose works intrigued the deputy in his youth continue to be cherished and reread on the eve of his death. This trait of the protagonist further identifies him as an authorial surrogate. In his diary, *Nero su nero*, Sciascia filters his daily experiences and thoughts through his 'strong reading' of a wide range of writers. The author often refers, as does the deputy, to the specific edition or translation in his possession, the physical condition of the book, and the frequency with which he rereads particular authors and texts.[10] The bookish protagonist's defence of rereading in the encounter with Signora De Matis echoes Leonardo Sciascia's own assessment of the importance of rereading as articulated in his essays. In 'Del rileggere' Sciascia moves away from the notion of the book as a fixed entity and towards a Borgesian concept of the text as part of a dynamic process. Citing Borges's story 'Pierre Menard, Author of Don Quixote,' he points out not only that the book's true existence lies in being read, but also and above all the mutability of that reading:

> Un libro non esiste in sé, e non soltanto per l'ovvio fatto che la sua vera esistenza, al di là della sua fisicità, consiste nell'esser letto, ma sopratutto perché è diverso per ogni generazione di lettori, per ogni singolo lettore e per lo stesso singolo lettore che torna a leggerlo. (*Opere*, 3:1221–2)

> A book does not exist on its own, and not only for the obvious reason that its true existence, beyond the physical realm, consists of being read, but above all because it is different for every generation of readers, for every single reader and for the same reader when he goes back to reread it.

As Sciascia suggests in this essay, and the deputy in his conversation with De Matis, the reader brings to bear on the reading of a book all that has passed since the last reading of the book, both her own personal experiences and society's experiences, 'nella storia umana.'

The deputy's evaluation of *Dead Souls*, particularly the 'open-ness' of Gogol's text to numerous readings, parallels Sciascia's own assessment. In 'Del rileggere' Sciascia comments at length on this very text as he articulates the importance of rereading and identifies the books most worthy of continued attention: *The Divine Comedy, Don Quixote, Hamlet*, and *Dead Souls*. Sciascia devotes the remainder of this essay to his reading of Gogol's text. He attributes the author's inability to complete *Dead Souls* to the depravity of the protagonist, Chichikov, who buys 'dead souls' in a profit-making scheme. Sciascia explains: 'la presenza stessa di Chichikov sommuove e rende evidente una corruzione vasta quanto l'impero, inesauribile' (*Opere*, 2:1223) [the very presence of Chichikov stirs up and makes evident the corruption as vast and inexhaustible as the empire]. He concludes that this desperate awareness of the ineradicable nature of corruption and injustice threatened to paralyse Gogol. Sciascia's own tragic sense of life is fully captured in his reading of Gogol's *Dead Souls*, a reading that undoubtedly coincides with the deputy's own.

The 'disperata consapevolezza' of Gogol represents one extreme in the deputy's state of mind in his dying days. This is underscored in chapter 7, where the narrator characterizes the Deputy's mood as one of profound pessimism and compares the protagonist to the Jewish secret service operative Rieti: 'Era come se nella loro mente ci fossero gli stessi circuiti, gli stessi processi logici. Computer della diffidenza, del sospetto, del pessimismo. Gli ebrei, i siciliani: atavica affinità della loro condizione' (*Opere*, 3:440) [It was as if the same circuits, the same logical processes operated in both their minds. A computer of distrust, of suspicion, of pessimism. Jews, Sicilians: an atavistic affinity in their condition] (*Knight*, 30). The deputy suffers on both a physical and a metaphysical level. As he contemplates the point at which he will no longer be able to tolerate the physical pain and will have to resort to morphine, the deputy draws the parallel with Giacomo Leopardi's 'uscir di pena è diletto fra noi': 'Belli gli effetti della morfina, più se succedevano all'insopportabile sofferenza. Più forte la tempesta, più dolce poi la quiete. *La quiete dopo la tempesta, Il sabato del villaggio, Il passero solitario, L'infinito*' (*Opere*, 3:452) [The effects of a morphine dose were wonderful, more so when they succeeded an intolerable level of pain. The stronger the storm the greater the peace. "Peace after the Storm," "Saturday in the Village," "The Solitary Sparrow," "Infinity"' (*Knight*, 42). The progress of the deputy's illness parallels the Leopardian resignation and despair into which he slowly sinks. That despair far exceeds the depiction of the defeat of reason in Sciascia's earlier *gialli*. The knowledge that he cannot save the world is eating at the deputy like a cancer.

Sciascia's protagonist bears a resemblance to the kindred spirits who suffer for the 'dolore del mondo offeso' in the conclusion of Vittorini's *Conversazione in Sicilia*. The pessimism of the protagonist and his friend Rieti is commensurate with the ineradicable and pervasive nature of the injustice they confront. The cancer that is causing the deputy to slowly waste away is almost a metaphysical response to the 'dolore del mondo offeso' and the cancer of absolute power. It remains to be seen whether such pessimism of cosmic dimensions will be born out in the conclusion of *Il cavaliere e la morte*. In the penultimate chapter of the novel the deputy returns to clear out his office in preparation for a medical leave that he anticipates will end in his death from cancer. The chief, who has carefully protected himself by pursuing 'the official story' in the Sandoz murder investigation, finally identifies with his dying colleague's quest for the truth: '"Mi dica la verità: lei voleva un mandato di cattura per Aurispa." Il fatto che lo chiamasse Aurispa, non più il Presidente, era invece segno che quel vagheggiamento ... era suo: un mandato di cattura per Aurispa' (*Opere*, 3:458) ['Tell me the truth: you wanted a warrant for Aurispa's arrest.' The fact that he now called him Aurispa and no longer the President was, none the less, a sign that he too felt, equally ardently, the same futile desire – to see a warrant issued for the arrest of Aurispa] (*Knight*, 47). While the chief now shares the deputy's thirst for the truth, this change of heart is articulated in the same breath in which both investigators recognize the futility of the quest. Implicit in the phrase 'he too felt ... the same futile desire' is the fact that the chief is recognized by the deputy as a kindred spirit. The deputy now sees in his superior another individual who shares his own desire to see justice served.

The focus of the closing pages of *Il cavaliere e la morte* shifts further and further from the murder mystery. If, as Barzun and Taylor have suggested, 'the detective story should be mainly occupied with detecting,' the lack of detecting in the second half of *Il cavaliere e la morte* should give the reader pause.[11] The deputy's mind is no longer on investigating the specific case at hand. Instead, as he departs from the office in which he has left behind his cherished Dürer engraving, he contemplates the ills of the past and the injustices of the future. He ponders the greatest evil of his own century, the Nazi concentration camps and the Holocaust, and speculates on the fate not only of the Children of '89, but also of the children of 1999, 2009, 2019. On the final day of his life the deputy awakens from a relatively pain-free night to read an article by the 'Great Journalist,' who has indeed published his accusation that the police and secret services have fostered the re-emergence of the cancer of terrorism as a scapegoat. The Great Journalist has, in other words, responded to the deputy's earlier challenge to reveal the truth and has published the deputy's suspicions. It appears that the protagonist's loss of faith in humankind is unwarranted.

During the last days of his life, the protagonist turns for solace to his favourite activity, rereading. After challenging the Great Journalist to publish the truth about the Sandoz murder, the deputy is overcome by weariness.

> Quel colloquio lo aveva innervosito, ma il dolore gli si era allontanato ... Poteva dunque, dall'ultima battuta di quel colloquio, vagheggiare l'isola deserta, come su una mappa svolgervi antico sogno, antica memoria; per quanto antiche gli erano diventate certe cose dell'infanzia, dell'adolescenza. *L'isola del tesoro*: una lettura, aveva detto qualcuno, che era quanto di più si poteva assomigliare alla felicità. Pensò: stasera lo rileggerò. (*Opere*, 3:448)

> [The conversation had left him drained, but the pain had gone ... The final words of the conversation, however, left him with a yearning for the deserted island, for a spot where, as though huddled over some map, he could give free rein to an ancient dream and an ancient memory: in as much as certain things from childhood and adolescence were now ancient to him. *Treasure Island*: a book, someone had said, which was the closest resemblance to happiness attainable. He thought: tonight I will re-read it.] (*Knight*, 38)

The deputy takes refuge on the desert island of Stevenson's masterpiece, a favourite childhood reading that stands in stark contrast to his adult reading of *Dead Souls*. Gogol's text, depicting the persistence of corruption and injustice, represents one extreme of the deputy's reading of the *liber mundi*. The opposite extreme is represented by his reading of *Treasure Island*, a book that, for the deputy, depicts the triumph of integrity and honour over greed and corruption.

The final scene of the novel abruptly shatters the utopian tranquility of the desert island. While rereading *Treasure Island*, the deputy is interrupted by his maid, who announces a breaking news item. Rieti, the secret service man who had confirmed the deputy's hypothesis of the president's guilt, has been shot and killed. 'Ora, prima che di pena, più che di pena, un sentimento di sconfitta lo agitava' (*Opere*, 3:464) [Now more than pain, stronger than pain, a feeling of defeat overcame him] (*Knight*, 53). As he is assailed by a metaphysical pain that overshadows the physical pain he suffers, the deputy hears the shots that will bring him eternal peace, the Leopardian 'quiete dopo la tempesta' that he had earlier contemplated: 'La vita se ne andava fluida, leggera; il dolore era scomparso. Al diavolo la morfina, pensò. E tutto era chiaro, già; Rieti era stato ucciso perché aveva parlato con lui' (*Opere*, 3:464–65) [Life was draining out of him, effortlessly, in a flow: the pain was no more. The hell with morphine, he thought. Everything was clear, now: Rieti had been murdered because he had spoken to him] (*Knight*, 53). The protagonist imagines the headlines in the next day's papers announcing that the Children of '89 have struck again and identifying the deputy as one of their victims. The truth of the deputy's murder at the hands of the shadowy conspirators concealed behind the Children of '89 will not be fully revealed in this life. The murder of the dying detective on the last page of *Il cavaliere e la morte* is an abrupt and shocking reminder to the reader that injustice often prevails. The conclusion of the novel marks a clear departure from the norms of the typical *romanzo poliziesco*. As Sciascia has pointed out, the reader of the traditional *giallo* is lulled into passivity:

> Il medio lettore di polizieschi, e cioè il miglior lettore di questo genere narrativo ... sa che la soluzione c'è già, alle ultimissime pagine ... e che il divertimento, il passatempo, consiste nella condizione – di assoluto riposo intellettuale – di affidarsi all'investigatore. (*Opere*, 2:1182)

> [The typical reader of detective novels, and that is the best reader of this type of narrative genre ... knows that the solution is already there, in the final pages ... and that the pleasure, the pastime, consists of the condition-of absolute intellectual repose – of entrusting oneself to the investigator.]

The intellectual repose described as the ideal mindset of the reader of the *giallo* is shattered in the conclusion to *Il cavaliere e la morte*. No typical *romanzo poliziesco*, *Il cavaliere e la morte* deprives the reader of the reassuring presence of the all-powerful investigator. Nonetheless, the fact that the deputy, the chief, Signora De Matis, and the Great Journalist know the truth and fight for justice provides some limited glimmer of hope. This conclusion is as optimistic as Sciascia can be at the end of his own life.

Like the deputy contemplating Dürer's engraving *The Knight, Death and the Devil*, Leonardo Sciascia was coming to grips with his own mortality in an unjust and imperfect world while writing *Il cavaliere e la morte*. The last lines of the novel can be ascribed not only to the protagonist but also to the author himself: 'Pensò: che confusione. Ma era già, eterno e ineffabile, il pensiero della mente in cui la sua si era sciolta' (*Opere*, 3:465) [He thought: what confusion! But it was now, eternally and ineffably, the thought of the mind into which his own had dissolved] (*Knight*, 54). The suggestion of the dissolving of his own power of thought into a supreme and eternal 'pensare' is the final hope that Sciascia's novel holds out to his reader. Perhaps others, like the various kindred spirits whom the deputy encounters in the course of his investigation – the chief, the Great Journalist, Signora De Matis, and even the reader – will come to embody that 'credo nella ragione umana' with which Leonardo Sciascia confronted the most intractable challenges of his time.

Both *Il cavaliere e la morte* and *Porte aperte* are constructed around what Umberto Eco calls 'un susurro di libri,' a whispered conversation in which books speak to other books.[12] Sciascia invites the reader to listen in on that whispered conversation, whether the literary work serves to expose the dystopian nature of the world or to provide an alternative, utopian model. Only with such nourishment can the reader begin to face up to life's challenges and redress society's ills. With his frequent references to cherished authors and dog-eared texts, from Gogol's indictment of the persistence of corruption in *Dead Souls* to Stevenson's portrayal of the triumph of good over evil in *Treasure Island*, the author draws the reader into his circle of kindred spirits. The weary knight of the Dürer engraving (and Sciasia's title) perhaps represents the writer himself at the moment when he must lay down the pen. His works will endure, however, to serve as a weapon to combat 'i mali del mondo offeso.'[13]

3 In Search of Isolina

Dacia Maraini's 1985 *Isolina: La donna tagliata a pezzi* is the story of an unsolved murder in turn-of-the-century Verona. Not a historical novel[1] but a meticulously researched inquiry into the miscarriage of justice in the case of the murder of a young woman, *Isolina* falls into the category of the *racconto inchiesta*.[2] The *inchiesta*, from Manzoni's *Storia della colonna infame* to Sciascia's *Morte dell'Inquisitore* to Maraini's *Isolina*, bears a great deal in common with the detective genre.[3] The process of 'ratiocination' through which the detective assembles the pieces of the puzzle parallels the process whereby the historian retrospectively reconstructs a series of past events.[4] Like a detective story, *Isolina* is composed of two stories, the story of the crime and the story of the investigation.[5] The story of the author's investigation into the Isolina case is as pivotal as the story of the murder itself. Maraini becomes a central character, a real–life detective who must solve a 'cold' case of an unsolved murder. But Maraini's is not simply an exercise in remote, archival research. Throughout the text the reader is reminded that the past continues to intrude upon the present; the unavenged murder and miscarriage of justice in the first year of the twentieth century relates to and informs our present moment. Maraini uses her considerable skills to solve the crime and to resurrect Isolina for the contemporary reader.

Isolina opens with the reconstruction of the gruesome crime. On 16 January 1900 two laundresses working on the banks of the Adige River in Verona notice a sack of what appears to be meat. Much to their horror, they discover it contains human remains. The next day the police drag the river for the remaining pieces of 'la donna tagliata a pezzi.' Two more bundles are discovered: one with the intestines of the victim, the other containing the oesophagus and a placenta with the umbilical cord still attached. It is determined that the victim was three months pregnant. As in Antonio Tabucchi's *La testa perduta di Damasceno Monteiro*, the head of the victim is missing, making positive identification difficult. Maraini reconstructs as much as possible about the crime from the documents, particularly the newspaper articles, of the period. All Verona became fascinated by the crime, which appeared to have been carried out by an 'expert hand.' From the missing person's report filed by one Felice Canuti, it was determined that the likely victim was Isolina Canuti, a nineteen-year-old girl whose character quickly came under intense scrutiny. Suspicion immediately fell on Carlo Trivulzio, a lieutenant in the *alpini*, or alpine regiment, and a boarder in the Canuti home. Lieutenant Trivulzio, of a noble and well-respected family, was considered by his fellow officers to be incapable of such a horrendous action. Inasmuch as the case quickly became a *cause célèbre*, Maraini is able to quote liberally from all of the newspapers, which followed the course of the investigation into the crime in morbid and vivid detail.

Maraini meticulously reconstructs the Isolina case, drawing upon every available document at her disposal, including police reports and photographs from local archives. To recreate the scene of the recovery of the body along the banks of the Adige, the author consults photographs from this period. The detail of the initial discovery 'sei pezzi di carne umana per il peso di kg 13,400' [six pieces of human flesh weighing 13.4 kg] is taken from the Veronese newspaper *L'Adige*. The initial questioning of Isolina's father, Felice Canuti, is quoted verbatim from *Il Corriere della Sera*. Maraini, however, bemoans the fact that the gaps in the historical record are daunting. There is no longer any trace of the lengthy interrogation of the victim's best friend, Maria Policante, called for questioning following Isolina's father. 'Ma pur-troppo non è rimasto niente, né all'Archivio di Stato, né al Tribunale, né alla Biblioteca di Verona. Tutto è stato distrutto, non si sa se per caso o deliberatamente' (*Isolina*, 10) [Unfortunately, no trace of these interrogations remains, either in the State Archives, or in the Court, or in the Library of Verona. Everything was destroyed. Accidentally? Deliberately?] (*Isolina*, 11). The detective work that went into the writing of *Isolina* begins to become evident in this authorial comment in chapter 1, which underscores the author's fruitless search for a missing document. In section 2 of *Isolina* Maraini will reveal the full extent of the investigative labour required to write the story of the crime. The degree of that labour equals the degree of the author's frustration at the gaps in the archival record. The speculation as to the cause of these gaps, whether by accident or design, will continue throughout *Isolina*.

The author/detective relies upon the indiscretions of the local newspapers of the time to fill in the gaps of the missing depositions. Maraini divides the newspapers into two categories: those that argue that the story against Trivulzio has been invented to discredit the military, and those that maintain that Trivulzio, if not the murderer, was at least an accomplice in the crime. Mario Todeschini, a socialist deputy in Parliament and editor-in-chief of the newspaper *Verona del popolo*, maintains that the evidence against Trivulzio is sufficient to warrant legal proceedings against him and accuses the authorities of a cover-up. Todeschini editorializes about the implications of the fact that the chief of police of Verona resigned his post after alluding to sinister forces interested in keeping the crime in the dark. The newspapers representing Verona's establishment, among them *L'Arena*, accuse Isolina of 'loose morals': 'Non era di irreprensibili costumi' (*Isolina*, 14) '[(Isolina) was not beyond reproach] (*Isolina*, 14). The socialist newspaper counters by accusing *L'Arena* of character defamation and appeals to the women of Verona to honour Isolina's memory and to commemorate her unburied remains.

The story of Maraini's investigation takes shape slowly as the story of the crime is introduced. The author assists the reader in sorting through the evidence as she reports the facts at her disposal. She quotes extensively from an interview with Lieutenant Trivulzio published in *Il Corriere della Sera* after his conditional release due to lack of evidence. Trivulzio admits to being Isolina's lover and admits that he knew she was pregnant. He denies, however, that he advised her to get an abortion and claims that he does not recognize the clothing on the victim's body. The author comments on this evasion:

> E qui Trivulzio fa un errore psicologico. La sua ostinazione nel non volere riconoscere l'identità del cadavere quando è stata confermata da tutti dimostra una eccessiva e palese voglia di allontanare da sé i sospetti nel modo più semplice, negando l'evidenza. (*Isolina*, 24)

> [Here Trivulzio made a psychological mistake. His stubborn refusal to recognize the body when everyone had confirmed that it was Isolina's was indicative of an extreme desire to deflect suspicion from himself in the simplest way possible, by denying the evidence.] (*Isolina*, 23)

This is one instance of an ongoing process in which the author helps the reader weigh and measure the veracity of the witnesses' accounts.

The operation of historical reconstruction undertaken in *Isolina* may be compared to another historical reconstruction by Leonardo Sciascia, *Morte dell'Inquisitore* (1964). In that work the author plays the role of the detective who assembles and interprets fragments of historical documents in an attempt to reconstruct the story of Fra Diego La Matina, a seventeenth-century Augustinian monk who was persecuted by the Inquisition and ultimately assassinated his inquisitor. Sciascia's *Morte dell'Inquisitore* was to some extent inspired by Alessandro Manzoni's *Storia della colonna infame*, the history of the alleged plague spreaders unjustly convicted and sentenced to death in Milan in 1630. Sciascia considered *Morte dell'Inquisitore* to be a continuation of the genre of the *racconto-inchiesta* initiated by Manzoni in *Storia della colonna infame*. In his introduction to the latter Sciascia expresses admiration for Manzoni's faithfulness to historical truth, 'l'intera e pura verità storica.' He was intrigued by the reasoning behind Manzoni's decision to expunge the historical 'digression' from *I promessi sposi* and to publish it first as an appendix to the novel and finally as a separate text. He cites a letter written by Manzoni to Adolphe de Circout, one of the few admirers of the book, in which Manzoni speaks of the pleasure that one feels upon being reassured that what seemed important to one's conscience was not entirely an illusion. Sciascia rejoins: '"Quel che è sembrato vero e importante alla coscienza." Alla sua coscienza, alla nostra. Alla nostra di oggi, alla nostra di fronte alla "cosa" e alle cose di oggi' ['That which seemed true and important to the conscience.' To his conscience, to our conscience, in the face of the 'things' of today] (21).'[6] Sciascia's denunciation of the persecution of innocent victims by the Inquisition in Sicily, like Manzoni's indictment of the infamous treatment of the alleged plague spreaders, is informed by the need to exercise moral judgment implied in the word 'conscience.'[7] The injustices of the past must be judged and condemned by the same moral code with which we judge the injustices of the present day, 'le cose di oggi.' *Isolina* is informed by the same sense of obligation. Maraini's painstaking attempt to uncover the injustices in the Isolina case stems from the same need to exercise moral judgment that motivated Sciascia and his predecessor Manzoni.

One of the tasks that most matters to Maraini is that of reconstructing an accurate portrait of the victim herself. As in *Voci*, where the detective, Michela Canova, attempts to 'flesh out' the victim, Angela Bari, so in *Isolina* the author tries to put a face on the headless victim.

Although there are no likenesses of Isolina, she is able to piece together the portrait of a nineteen-year-old about whom certain facts are known: Isolina was affectionate and vivacious, loved to dance, and adored sweet mustard. From the sister's testimony at the later trial, the author concludes that Isolina wanted to keep her unborn child. From the detail that Isolina sold a ring inherited from her mother in order to purchase marsala and eggs to concoct a *zabaione* for her lover, she deduces that Isolina was indeed in love with Lieutenant Trivulzio. As we learn how Isolina had cared for her friend Maria Policante after Maria's abortion, the author comments: 'Possiamo immaginarla, con le sue gonne lunghe scarlatte, il passo leggero, che si dirige veloce verso la casa della levatrice con un fagotto appeso al braccio' (*Isolina*, 29) [Let us imagine her, with her long scarlet skirt, her light step taking her quickly towards the midwife's house with a bundle in her arms] (*Isolina*, 27). In the first person plural of *possiamo* the author addresses the reader and enlists his or her participation in the task of resurrecting the vivacious, fun-loving, and kind-hearted Isolina. There emerges an image of a flesh-and-blood young woman to whom the author, and the reader, may relate and whose loss the reader can only mourn.

Section 2, entitled 'Sulle trace di Isolina,' focuses not only on the victim but also on the author/historian and the story of the investigation in which she has engaged. The presence of the author is announced in the opening paragraph: 'Arrivo il 19 settembre col treno di Roma' (*Isolino*, 49) [I arrive Thursday, 19 September, on the train from Rome] (*Isolina*, 43). Accompanied by her friend Pippo Zappulla, one of her creative writing students,[8] the author tries to revisit the scene of the crime. Pippo introduces her to many new Veronese friends who will assist her in the investigation. The story of Maraini's investigation includes a colourful cast of real-life characters: the contagiously optimistic lawyer avvocato Guariendi; the affable and refined Sicilian Sebastiano Livoti, president of the Tribunal; the courteous director of the Archivio di Stato. No matter where the author turns, however, she is thwarted in her investigation. The restaurant Il chiodo that in all likelihood was the scene of the gruesome crime is no longer standing. She is unable to find a trace of the files of the preliminary investigation into the murder. Nor is any trace of the victim's remains found. Yet it is this very 'disappearing' of Isolina that strengthens the author in her resolve to make the victim's presence felt.[9]

As the author follows in Isolina's footsteps, she begins to refer to her investigation as 'il mio pellegrinaggio' [my pilgrimage]. Maraini's choice of words reflects the quasi-religious fervour with which she pursues her task. During a visit to the Verona cemetery, the author finds neither a headstone commemorating Isolina's short span of life nor any file regarding the disposition of her remains. She surmises that Isolina's bones must lie in the cemetery's communal grave.

> Ma le ossa rimangono, anche ridotte a pezzetti, a testimonianza di un corpo che una volta è stato vivo contro ogni volontà di annullamento continuando a dare segno di sé in silenzio ma con decisione come a dire: ci sono voluti nove mesi per darmi una forma, ci sono voluti anni e anni per fare di me una persona adulta, anni di lavoro, di amore, di sonno, di cibo, e non puoi, semplicemente non puoi eliminarmi. (*Isolina*, 53)

> [But the bones still remain, reduced to little pieces, as testimony to a body which was once alive despite every desire to annihilate it, and which continues to signal silently but decisively as if to say: It took nine months to give me form, it took years and years to make me an adult, years of work, of love, of sleep, of nourishment, and you cannot, you simply cannot eliminate me.] (*Isolina*, 47)

The author becomes a kind of medium through which the victim herself speaks from the communal grave.

Maraini's insistent and very personal 'presence' in her historical text is in direct contrast to the absence of the author in classical histories. From Herodotus to Machiavelli to Michelet, the historian suppresses any sign of his or her presence in order to maintain the illusion of objectivity. The less he or she intrudes in the text, the more the veracity of the text is assured. As Roland Barthes has pointed out, however, the absence of the historian from the text is an illusion.[10] The historian is always behind the scenes, sifting through the 'facts,' carving them up and assembling them in a manner that cannot help but reveal the presence of the author. In Maraini's history of Isolina, as in Sciascia's *Morte dell'Inquisitore*, the fiction of the author's absence is discarded. The author/historian periodically reminds the reader of her presence. We follow in Maraini's footsteps as she combs the city of Verona looking for any clue to the mystery of Isolina. The author patiently searches the city archives, but to no avail: 'Per i registi comunali non è mai esistita' (*Isolina*, 55) [As far as the community registers go, she never existed] (*Isolina*, 48). She writes of her visit to the convent school where Isolina boarded for several years and of her frustration when she has no luck gaining further information regarding Isolina. Yet she is able to deduce much of the daily rhythm of Isolina's life when she realizes that the convent school is remarkably similar to the one in Florence where she herself spent three years of her adolescence. Where the historical record fails, the author's implicit identification with Isolina gives her insight into the victim's 'piccolo mondo femminile' (61). Maraini reports on her visit to the barracks of the alpini, with its opulent decor and eighteenth-century paintings, and comments on the overwhelming air of privilege: 'Il sentimento di appartenza ad una casta eletta si respira nell'aria' (*Isolina*, 62) [You can breathe this feeling of belonging to a special caste in the very air] (*Isolina*, 54). Throughout the pages reporting on her pilgrimage, the author begins to question her motives for remaining in Verona, where the trail of Isolina's footsteps has gone cold. As she returns, exhausted, to her room in vicolo Chiodo, the street on which, the restaurant Il chiodo, the scene of the crime, once stood, she comments 'Mi sembra di non riuscire ad afferrare il senso di questa ricerca che pure mi affascina e mi intriga' (*Isolina*, 63) [It seems to me that I fail to understand the meaning of this search which nevertheless continues to intrigue and fascinate me] (*Isolina*, 54). Despite the investigative skill with which she pursues Isolina's story, Maraini is unable fully to grasp the reason for her own obsession with the murder case.

She provides a partial answer to this question in *Amata scrittura*, a volume of essays inspired by her encounters with both aspiring and established writers. In a dialogue with her peers entitled 'Scrivere per ...,' the author lists in the subtitles of the essay ('Scrittura come terapia,' 'Scrittura come rimedio contro la solitudine,' etc.) a number of reasons why the writer takes up the pen. Under the heading 'Scrittura e memoria' Maraini explores the ways in which writing allows the author to 'untie the knots of the past' ('sciogliere i nodi del passato,' 87). Even when writing non-fiction inspired by a 'fatto di cronaca,' the author is moved by a profoundly personal motivation.

> Anche quando accoglie nella sua mente una storia che gli è estranea, un fatto di cronaca, dei personaggi lontani nel tempo e nello spazio, le ragioni per cui si approfondisce questa storia, per cui si sofferma con materna inquietudine sul corpo dei protagonisti, sono sempre profondamente personali e interiori. (88)

> [Even when she receives in her mind a story which is extraneous to her, characters who are far away in space and time, the reasons for which she

develops this story, for which she dwells with maternal uneasiness on the body of the protagonists, are always profoundly personal and interior.

Later in the same essay, Maraini mentions *Isolina* in the same breath with Sciascia's documentary work on the mafia. The profoundly personal nature of Maraini's inquiry becomes more and more apparent in 'Sulle trace di Isolina' ['In Isolina's Footsteps']. The more the character eludes Maraini during the day, the more she haunts her by night. The author is tormented in her sleep by images of rivers flooded with women's bodies. The dream provides a key to Maraini's personal and interior motivation. She is not only determined to bring Isolina alive for the reader as a unique, flesh-and-blood nineteen-year-old. As the dream of the river swollen with women's bodies suggests, Isolina comes to symbolize all victims of violence against women.

'Sulle trace di Isolina' ends as Maraini assembles the pieces of the puzzle to the best of her ability and fills in the gaps left by the missing elements. In the absence of key documents such as the depositions by the prime suspect and key witnesses at the preliminary investigation, the author must use other means to discover the truth. She draws conclusions regarding the perpetrator of the crime and the role of Trivulzio that are based on an informed sixth sense rather than on hard evidence. 'Probabilmente ... Trivulzio fu a cena con gli altri ufficiali ma l'iniziativa di far abortire Isolina non fu sua' (*Isolina*, 82) [Probably ... Trivulzio did have supper that famous evening with some other officers, but the initiative to make Isolina abort was not his] (*Isolina*, 69). The author surmises that Isolina died in a botched abortion and that one of the officers then decided to dismember her ('farla a pezzi') in order to destroy the evidence of the crime. According to this theory, Trivulzio, out of a misguided sense of honour, did not want to incriminate a fellow officer. The author reads Trivulzio's death of stomach cancer as a symptom of the gnawing regret that slowly ate away at the lieutenant following this act of *omertà*.

The penultimate section of *Isolina*, dealing with the trial of Todeschini, reads like the script of a courtroom drama in which each of the participants one by one takes center stage. Todeschini, the socialist deputy and editor of *Verona del Popolo*, kept the case alive in the pages of his newspaper after the release of Trivulzio, and was ultimately charged with defamation of character. The author sets the scene with vivid descriptions of the witnesses based upon the sketches of the court artist. In reconstructing this section of Isolina's story, she has access to the full transcript of the trial testimony. Missing are the proceedings of the preliminary investigation into Isolina's murder. Just as the defence attorneys are hampered in their defense of Onorevole Todeschini by lack of access to the records of the preliminary murder investigation, so Maraini is hindered by this highly suspicious gap. Nonetheless, the records of the Todeschini defamation trial provide ample evidence. The first to appear on the witness stand is Trivulzio. Maraini liberally cites the words of the plaintiff and marvels at the fact that he admits everything short of direct responsibility for Isolina's death. Following the lengthy report of Trivulzio's testimony, the author reports the testimony of Isolina's father, sister, and best friend, and other key witnesses.

Maraini closes each scene with an authorial comment on the value of the testimony re-enacted for the reader. Isolina's sixteen-year-old sister, Clelia Canuti, testifies that Trivulzio was Isolina's lover, that Isolina confided in her sister that she was pregnant, and that Trivulzio had given Isolina a substance to induce a miscarriage. She also testifies to a previous affair of Isolina's, offering unnecessarily graphic detail to the delight of Trivulzio's lawyers. The author concludes:

> Come si vede Clelia era di un candore che a momenti rasenta la deficienza. Una bambina impaurita che cerca di compiacere i giudici e non conosce l'effetto delle cose che dice. Non pensa nemmeno a salvare la sorella. Basterebbero poche sue parole per perdere Trivulzio. Ma lei non le dice. E questo dimostra fin troppo chiaramente che le cose che rivela sono solo la verità. (*Isolina*, 107)

> [It is evident that Clelia was sometimes candid to the point of half-wittedness. A frightened child who was trying to please the judges, and did not realize the effect of the things she was saying. She did not even think of protecting her sister. It would have taken very few words on her part to damn Trivulzio. But she didn't say them. And this finally showed only too clearly that the things she did reveal were the truth.] (*Isolina*, 91)

The potentially damning nature of the sister's graphic testimony about Isolina's first lover and her failure to directly accuse Trivulzio paradoxically lead the author to put the stamp of truth on Clelia's testimony. This type of authorial intervention constitutes a particular instance of what Roland Barthes calls the monitorial mode, which he defines as one 'which combines a message (the event reported), a code-statement (the informer's contribution) and a message about the code-statement (the author's evaluation of his source)' ('Historical discourse,' 146). Maraini's historical reconstruction, like Sciascia's *Morte dell'Inquisitore*, relies heavily on the monitorial mode.

Maraini filters and monitors the testimony of the key witnesses throughout her account of the defamation trial. She finds particularly revealing the testimony of the former editor of *Gazzettino di Verona*, Alessandro Carlini, regarding Trivulzio's role in the crime. The journalist testifies in court that De Mori, a midwife, told him in an interview the name of the lieutenant who had sent Isolina to her for an abortion: Trivulzio. According to the journalist, she claimed to have written 'Tribulzio' on her wall so as not to forget the name. Carlini testifies that two police officers he questioned while investigating the case for *Gazzettino di Verona* corroborated De Mori's story. When questioned in court on the veracity of De Mori's account, however, the officers deny having seen Trivulzio's misspelled name on the midwife's wall. A third party whom Carlini had asked to hide in an armoire to listen to the police officers' account corroborates the journalist's story. The author comments in bemused awe on Carlini's ingenuity: 'E qui si trasforma addirittura in un investigatore da libro giallo' (*Isolina*, 121) [At this point the situation begins to sound like something out of a detective novel] (*Isolina*, 103). Maraini recounts Carlini's clever ruse with admiration for his detective skills and absolute conviction that he is on the right track. It is important to note her keen regard for the figure of the young journalist who doggedly uncovers the truth. In opposition to the bulk of the sensationalistic coverage, which distorts the truth and exploits the victim (whether in establishment or opposition newspapers, whether for or against Trivulzio), stand isolated examples of investigative journalism of the highest order. The work of the young Carlini falls into the latter category. The journalist who rises above the usual tactics of the tabloids embodies the power of the fourth estate when used in a socially responsible manner.[11]

The process whereby the author/historian collects, evaluates, and assembles the data is laid bare in this section of *Isolina*. She endorses some testimony as plausible and discards some as patently false. The author judges that it is worthwhile ('vale la pena') to cite verbatim the testimony of the ex-police chief, Cacciatori, who handled the original case in which Trivulzio, although not exonerated, was released for lack of evidence. She allows the police chief's verbatim testimony to tell much of the story. Cacciatori testifies that he was convinced at the time of the initial investigation that Trivulzio was implicated in the crime and that nothing has occurred to change his mind. Maraini guides the reader through the process of evaluating the police chief's testimony and drawing the correct conclusions. Cacciatori had to reconcile his duty as a civil servant and his duty to his own convictions. He denies receiving any pressure from the military authorities during his handling of the case, but at the same time refuses to contradict a witness who testifies to having heard the judge complain of interference from above. The author concludes: 'Per fare questo non si sottrae alle più ardite acrobazie: nega di avere ricevuto delle pressioni dalle autorità militari ma nello stesso tempo si rifiuta di dare del bugiardo a chi ha testimoniato di averglielo sentito dire' (*Isolina*, 125) [To do this he performed the most daring acrobatics: he denied that he had ever been pressured by the military authorities while at the same time he refused to call someone a liar – even when he had actually given evidence that they had lied] (*Isolina*, 106). Maraini guides the reader through this process to gain the reader's concurrence with her evaluation of the witness and to lead the reader to the correct conclusion. The most plausible explanation for the witness's conflicting testimony, she argues persuasively, is that the police chief was under pressure from the military authorities to protect the reputation of the *alpini* and to drop the charges against Trivulzio.

The presence of the author, which might at first lead to an impression of lack of objectivity, ultimately reminds the reader that history does not write itself, that all histories are 'constructions.' As Hayden White has observed, historiography is 'ineluctably interpretive,' 'as much a "making" (*inventio*) as ... a "finding" of the facts that comprise the structure of its perceptions' (285).[12] The important question is the solidity of that construction. In the case of Sciascia's *Morte dell'Inquisitore*, the author lays bare the constructive principles that have allowed him to fabricate his story in the hope that the reader will be convinced of the solidity of that construct. Maraini's insistent presence functions in much the same manner in *Isolina*. She lays bare the process through which she forges the links in her reconstruction of the case in order to win the reader's concurrence.

The author becomes increasingly judgmental as she reports on the conclusion of the Todeschini trial. In the summations, the plaintiff's attorneys argue that the case against Trivulzio has been trumped up as part of a socialist plot to discredit the military. Trivulzio is portrayed by his attorneys as an upstanding officer and an innocent victim: 'In che brutto ambiente è caduto il povero Trivulzio ignaro di ogni cosa!' (*Isolina*, 158) [Trivulzio, who was completely innocent, found himself in this ugly situation!] (*Isolina*, 132). The notion that Trivulzio was unwittingly seduced by his landlord's wayward daughter falls into the age-old pattern of incriminating the victim rather than the perpetrators of crimes against women.[13] The attorney's claim that Lieutenant Trivulzio was in bed reading D'Annunzio while unsuccessfully warding off Isolina's advances is as laughable as it is implausible. As Maraini points out, all witnesses testifying against Trivulzio are characterized by attorneys for the plaintiff as either politically motivated or 'nevropatico.' 'Questa parola "nevropatico" piace molto all'avvocato Pagani-Cesa che la usa contro tutti quelli le cui testimonianze possono danneggiare Trivulzio' (*Isolina*, 149) [These words 'pathological neurotic case' appealed to the lawyer Pagani-Cesa very much and he used them against anyone whose evidence could be damaging to Trivulzio] (*Isolina*, 125). The defence attorneys argue that there is a great deal of circumstantial evidence pointing to Trivulzio as an accomplice in the crime. And so, they conclude, their client cannot be considered guilty of character assassination. Having evaluated and found credible the testimony of Isolina's sister, father, and best friend in addition to that of the journalist Carlini and the ex-police chief, Cacciatore, Maraini leads the reader to concur with the defence. On the basis of the testimony reported, Todeschini's suspicion of Trivulzio is eminently reasonable. The author reports a portion of the defence attorney's summation referring to the possibility that this case might one day inspire a novel: 'Gli indizi contro Trivulzio oggettivamente erano gravi e questi indizi non sono mutati in un anno di tempo ... Se un romanziere un giorno avesse a scrivere intorno a questo fatto dovrebbe intitolare il primo suo capitolo "un muro che parla"' (*Isolina*, 163) [Seen objectively, the evidence against Trivulzio was serious and this evidence remains unchanged a year later ... If one day a novelist were to write about what happened, he might entitle his first chapter: 'The wall which spoke'] (*Isolina*, 136). It is almost as if Maraini has taken up the pen in response to the defence attorney's invitation.

The final section of *Isolina* tells the story of the outcome of the Todeschini trial. The author reports the sentence without comment. The socialist deputy Todeschini is found guilty of defamation of character and sentenced to twenty-three months of imprisonment and a fine of 1,458 lire. Maraini provides excerpts from all of the newspapers reporting on the sentence while initially suppressing her own comment. The reader at this point fully comprehends the miscarriage of justice in this case. Having guided the reader towards the truth, the author does not need to denounce this outcome as unjust. Not only was Todeschini falsely accused and convicted. More importantly, Isolina was maligned in the trial and wronged by the sentence. Finally, Trivulzio, in all likelihood an accomplice if not the perpetrator of the crime, goes unpunished. Maraini's silence on this outcome speaks louder than any words. The only intrusion of the author in this chapter is the comment that the newspapers, whether for or against Todeschini, have once again managed to make the victim disappear. 'Nessuno si ricorda di Isolina, Il solo giornale che ne fa cenno è "La Libertà" di Padova, che scrive: "Tutto questo purtroppo non è servito allo scopo principale cioè quello di fare luce sull'assassinio di Isolina Canuti"' (*Isolina*, 170) [No one remembered Isolina. The only newspaper that mentioned her was *La Libertà* in Padua which wrote: 'All this unfortunately has not helped the main objective, which was to shed light on the murder of Isolina Canuta'] (*Isolina*, 142). It is in order to reverse this 'disappearing act' and shed light on Isolina's murder that Maraini has taken up her pen.[14]

In the final chapter of *Isolina* the author allows herself to pass judgment on the judges in the Todeschini trial: 'Hanno una grande abilità questi giudici nel dire senza dire, nel narrare senza narrare, nel giudicare senza prendere posizione' (*Isolina*, 176) [These judges had an enormous talent for saying a great deal without saying anything, for telling a story with no content, for making a judgment without taking a stand] (*Isolina*, 148). Maraini exposes the hypocrisy of the judges, who discredit all witnesses, despite the preponderance of evidence, except those who testify to the 'loose morals' of Isolina. She ridicules the manoeuvring through which they try to exclude the possibility that Trivulzio could be the father of the victim's unborn child. The contrast between the judges' defamation of Isolina's character and their magnanimous treatment of Trivulzio is particularly repugnant to Maraini. The author drives home the point that Trivulzio and Isolina are not equal before the law. The victim, as so often occurs in cases of violence against women, is found guilty: 'Isolina Canuti, si legge fra le righe, se l'è voluta' (*Isolina*, 182) [You can read between the lines that they were saying Isolina got what she asked for] (*Isolina*, 152). The author concludes by calling attention to the 'fictionality' of the sentence: 'Così si conclude il processo Todeschini con una sentenza che sembra finta tanto è teatralmente di parte' (*Isolina*, 182) [And so Todeschini's trial concluded with a sentence that seems farcical because it was so obviously one-sided] *(Isolina,* 152). Maraini's indictment of the judges charged with upholding justice places them at centre stage in what Sciascia called 'la storia del disonore umana.'[15]

Maraini's *Isolina* is a meticulous historical reconstruction of a notorious murder case and a cautionary tale about violence against women in patriarchal society. It is also the account of the writer's successful crusade to bring the story to light. The story of the brutal murder of Isolina and the miscarriage of justice in the case is implicitly presented as relevant and valuable to the contemporary reader. As the author shifts from Isolina's past to our present, from the crime of violence against women in turn-of-the-century Verona to the investigation into that crime from the perspective of the end of the twentieth century, the ideological implications of the story of Isolina are underscored. Maraini's text is a powerful example of what Hayden White calls ethical interpretation in history, in which the object of study is 'not "history" per se or "the past" in general, but rather the social matrix experienced as an extension out of the past into the writer's present' (305). The implication is that the representation of the story of Isolina can shed light on the present day. Just as in Sciascia's *Morte dell'Inquisitore* the author is interested not only in crimes of the Spanish Inquisition in sixteenth-century Sicily but in inquisitions of all sorts, so Maraini is interested not only in the isolated case of Isolina but in violence against women wherever and whenever it occurs. *Isolina*, together with Maraini's 1994 *Voci*, constitutes an eloquent and impassioned indictment of the victimization of women. Whether set in contemporary Rome, as in *Voci*, or turn-of-the-century Verona, whether based on archival research or fictionalized, Maraini's companion texts bring the victims alive and move the reader to denounce the as-yet unsolved crime of violence against women.

4 *Voci* and the Conventions of the *Giallo*

With her acclaimed 1994 novel *Voci*, Dacia Maraini draws upon the most codified and conventional of genres, the detective novel, to produce an unconventional and highly original work of fiction.[1] Like the detective fiction of Leonardo Sciascia and Antonio Tabucchi, Maraini's novel exploits the conventions of the classical *giallo* while departing from many of those conventions in interesting and significant ways. From the *modus operandi* of the two detectives to the mode of narration to the solution of the crime, the author plays with and upsets the norms of the typical *romanzo poliziesco*. While Sciascia employed the detective genre both to critique political corruption in Italy and to denounce abuses of power wherever they occur, Maraini uses the genre to expose another pervasive and equally troubling scourge of contemporary society: the scandalous number of unsolved crimes against women in Italy and in Western society. The novel is a gripping exposé of a problem that has occupied Maraini for at least a decade. The author has remarked on the inspiration behind *Voci* in the 1995 interview *Conversazione con Dacia Maraini*: 'Nel caso di *Voci* ... il suo germe sta nella ricerca che per anni ho portato avanti sui delitti contro le donne' (30) [In the case of *Voci*, the inspiration lies in the research that I have conducted for years on crimes against women]. Maraini's research has taken her to turn-of-the-century Verona, scene of the unsolved murder at the heart of her non-fiction novel *Isolina: La donna tagliata a pezzi* (1992). Most recently, it has resulted in the publication of *Buio* (1999), winner of the prestigious Premio Strega, a volume composed of twelve stories of sexual violence against women and children that takes its departure from recent news reports. The fictional police officer investigating the actual crimes featured in *Buio* is the same

Inspector Adele Sòfia who makes her first appearance in Maraini's *Voci*.

Voci features two female detectives, Michela Canova and Adele Sòfia, one amateur and one professional. Michela, the narrator, is a journalist who works for a radio station in Rome. As the novel opens, she returns from an assignment to find that her neighbour, Angela Bari, has been brutally murdered by an unknown party. The discovery of the corpse not only triggers an investigation by the authorities. It also sparks in Michela the desire to take on the role of detective and bring the culprit to justice. On the same day that she learns of the murder of Angela Bari, the journalist is assigned to develop a series on unsolved crimes against women for her radio station. This assignment begins to overlap with her growing involvement in the Angela Bari case. At the outset of her investigation Michela is referred to Adele Sòfia, the police inspector in charge of the crime unit and, ultimately, of the Bari case.

In accordance with the conventions of the classical, English-style detective novel, *Voci* unfolds within a relatively closed society.[2] The milieu is composed of a group of apparently innocent individuals who one by one come under suspicion. The narrator interviews each of the primary suspects and witnesses in the course of the novel. The *dramatis personae* include the victim's lover, Giulio Carlini, mother, stepfather, sister, sister's boyfriend, and a pimp by the name of Nando Pepi. The journalist's interviews with these suspects are captured on tape as so many 'voci,' as reflected in the title of the novel. At first, it seems to Michela as if she is making no progress in the investigation: 'Non so niente di niente. Più vado avanti e meno capisco. Buio completo' (*Voci*, 121) [I know absolutely nothing. The deeper I go into it the less I understand. I'm totally in the dark] (*Voices*, 97). The narrator's uncertainty is mirrored quite effectively in the mode of narration itself. As Todorov has pointed out in 'Typologie du roman policier,' the classical detective novel makes a clear distinction between the story of the crime and the story of the investigation.[3] The classical *giallo*, from Edgar Alan Poe onward, is narrated in the past tense. The story of the investigation is told retrospectively from a triumphant present when the truth has been uncovered. In Maraini's *Voci*, by contrast, the story of the investigation is in the present tense. The steps in the investigation are narrated as they occur, not retrospectively. This mode of narration is atypical and disorienting, signalling to the reader that the outcome is uncertain. The reassurance afforded by the retrospective certainty of the classical detective story is here withheld by the author.

The key to the solution of the murder mystery lies in understanding the character of the victim. The character of Angela Bari emerges slowly as the narrator questions the victim's mother, sister, various lovers, and stepfather. There emerges a composite portrait of a child-woman, sweet and submissive, by some accounts seductive, difficult and capricious by others. The contradictory testimony contributes to the development of a distinct character type, one that Maraini has come to recognize. In a 1995 interview the author explained that, out of the reams of material she has collected on crimes against women, there has emerged a profile that she identifies with the victim, a type of woman who opens the door to her assassin: 'È come se nel destino di una donna che punta tutto sulla seduzione ci sia segnato anche quello possibile di vittima da intender in senso ampio' (*Conversazione con Dacia Maraini*, 31) [It is as if, in the destiny of a woman who stakes everything on seduction, there is also the possible destiny of the victim to be understood in a broad sense]. Angela Bari is the embodiment of this character type. Unlike the typical *giallo*, *Voci* does not exploit the corpse on page one as a simple device to set the plot in motion.[4] The playfulness with which the classical detective story treats the victim, the body in the library, is replaced in Maraini's *Voci* by dead earnestness. The victim remains at centre stage throughout the novel, reminding the reader of a problem that lies, in Maraini's words, 'alle radici più profonde della nostra cultura' (*Conversazione*, 31) [at the deepest roots of our culture].

A necessary ingredient in the formula for detective fiction is not only the presence of a mystery, a riddle, but also the drive to solve the riddle. Both the narrator and the police inspector are animated by the same need that lies at the heart of the classical *giallo*: 'il bisogno tutto umano e tutto profondo di risolvere un enigma' (*Voci*, 34) [the deep and altogether human need to resolve a riddle] (*Voices*, 25). In the classical detective story it is the male detective who satisfies this human need and provides what Barzun calls 'the spectacle of the human mind at work' (22). At issue in any *giallo* that features a female detective is whether the detective who solves the riddle will be androgynous or whether she will display (stereotypically) female characteristics. Some feminist scholars argue that the balancing act between the scripts of 'woman' and 'detective' is so difficult that novelists featuring female detectives have had to choose between one script or the other, such that their 'character was either not a proper detective or not a proper woman' (Klein, 3).[5] Heilbrun has taken a somewhat different approach to the question, pointing out that, whether written by a male or a female, the classical English detective novel has always boasted androgynous males like Sherlock Holmes and Hercule Poirot. The author belittles those detective novels in which sexual stereotyping plays a prominent role, and in particular dismisses the work of the 'hard-boiled' detective writers (Hammett, Chandler, and Macdonald). She heralds a new age of writers, male and female, who have begun to challenge sexual stereotyping. Heilbrun welcomes the creation by female writers of androgynous female detectives and concludes with the claim that the detective genre at its best has a kind of subversive power: 'I think that this openness about the prison of gender is one of the detective novel's great claims to fame' ('Gender and Detective Fiction,' 7).

Heilbrun is unquestionably correct in focusing on the importance of the gender/genre relationship in detective fiction. While Maraini's characters do not fit easily into either of the molds described by Heilbrun, it is interesting to consider her female detectives, Adele Sòfia and Michela Canova, in light of the classical models of the detective. Adele bears some similarity to Auguste Dupin, Sherlock Holmes, and Hercule Poirot, the classical, androgynous male sleuths preferred by Heilbrun. Barzun describes the literary descendant of Poe's Dupin as 'a man of independent mind, an eccentric possibly, something of an artist even in his "scientific" work, and in any case a creature of will and scope superior to the crowd' (22). Maraini's lesbian Inspector Adele Sòfia exhibits the same kind of cool mastery that characterizes her fictional predecessors. She is a poet who relies upon scientific methods of criminology that she patiently explains to Michela. Just as Watson calls the reader's attention to Holmes's remarkable intellectual power, so Michela admires the police inspector's intellectual prowess and views her as a superior being: 'La guardo mettersi in piedi con maestà. Tutto in lei comunica tranquillità, pazienza, robustezza mentale ... si muove con perfetto equilibrio in mezzo ai morti sbudellati, ... con quella fredda passione per 'i teoremi da dimostrare' che la anima' (*Voci*, 135) [I watch her getting up on to her feet with dignity. Everything about her gives a feeling of calm, patience and mental vigour ... she moves with perfect equilibrium among the butchered corpses, the slaughtered bodies with a cold passion for the 'theorems of proof' that animated her] (*Voices*, 110). Although Adele's mastery and cool passion, as seen through the eyes of Michela, conjure up a Sherlock Holmes, Auguste

Dupin, or Hercule Poirot, unlike these classical sleuths the inspector does not fall into the category of androgynous detective.

Adele Sòfia's maternal characteristics clearly mark her as female. The narrator underscores her maternal side on more than one occasion. Adele, as seen through the eyes of the narrator, is 'materna nei movimenti' (*Voci*, 49) [maternal in her movements]. As Adele cites the statistics on violence against women with detached competence, Michela notes in her 'la stessa matronale potenza' (50) [the same matronly presence] (*Voices*, 38) of a Gertrude Stein. The inspector explains the details of DNA testing to the narrator 'con pazienza materna' (131) [with maternal patience]. Despite her cool professionalism, generally associated with the male detective, Adele is repeatedly shown as maternal and nurturing. Most of the conversations between the narrator and Adele Sòfia take place as Sòfia prepares or serves dinner. The narrator marvels at the duality of Adele's character: 'Con quelle dita che conoscono la plasticità dei cibi, stringe le manette ai polsi degli assassini ... Che sia proprio della scienza materna questo mescolare ... il nutriente al castigante' (*Voci*, 153) [with those fingers that are so familiar with the tactile quality of food, she clasps handcuffs on to the wrists of murderers. A mixture of softness and hardness, of nurture and punishment – the attributes of a mother] (*Voices*, 125). Rather than showing Adele Sofia's maternal side and her castigating side as contradictory 'scripts,' the narrator speculates that these may be complementary. Michela not only admires Adele's 'mente fredda,' her professional competence, but also her matronly ways. Initially, it seems that the inspector will become Michela's 'symbolic mother' (*madre simbolica*) an older, more powerful woman to whom the younger woman turns in a relationship of entrustment (*affidamento*), as described by Italian feminists.[6] 'As a guiding concept of feminist practice, in the relationship of entrustment [*affidamento*], the notion of the symbolic mother permits the exchange between women across generations and the sharing of knowledge and desire across difference ... It enables ... the alliance "between the woman who wants and the woman who knows," that is to say, a mutual valorization of the younger woman's desire for recognition and self-affirmation in the world, and the older woman's knowledge of female symbolic defeat in the social-symbolic world designed by men' (de Lauretis, 11). While the relationship between Michela and Adele Sòfia initially seems to correspond to this model, ultimately that relationship develops in more complex, and less predictable, ways.

Although in many respects the two are a study in contrasts, neither

Adele nor Michela conforms to the convention of the androgynous female detective. Carolyn Heilbrun, as we have seen, sees as a positive move the creation of androgynous female sleuths who escape the sexual stereotyping prevalent in society at large. Maraini rejects this solution and creates two highly nuanced, fully developed female characters whose 'femaleness' plays a role in solving the crime. As the narrator, Michela cannot provide an objective characterization of herself. The reader must draw her own conclusions about Michela as the novel, and the investigation, proceed. A professional woman and something of a loner, she hates to cook, often forgets to eat, and is generally shown eating alone. She is perceived by others, such as Avvocato Merli, as 'laboriosa, disciplinata, autonoma' (*Voci*, 202) [hard-working, disciplined, self-reliant] (*Voices*, 166). Despite obvious signs of Michela's competence, she has moments of self-doubt. These are reinforced by repeated references to her as 'imbranata' [incompetent], first by an unknown male driver who calls her 'imbranata come tutte le donne' (32).[7] In her article on gender and detective fiction Heilbrun quotes the transsexual Jan Morris, who gives an example of sexual stereotyping that is strikingly similar to the incident recounted in Maraini's novel: 'The more I was treated as a woman, the more woman I became. If I was assumed to be incompetent at reversing cars, or opening bottles, oddly incompetent I found myself becoming' (5). It is this very stereotype of the woman perceived as incompetent, whether at driving in reverse or solving mysteries, that Michela resists early in the novel. Later she is called 'imbranata' by her colleague Tirinnanzi, who is peeved by her unwillingness to fight the station manager when he threatens to take her off the story. The same term is used by Angela Bari's sister to describe the victim of the crime (34). Michela is struck by this apparent coincidence. It becomes only the first piece of a larger pattern in which the narrator gradually comes to identify with the victim.

Michela and the victim are by all appearances also a study in contrasts. Avvocato Merli suggests to Michela that Angela would not have singled her out were it not for the fact that she viewed Michela as her opposite. The author indeed speaks of Michela and Angela as polar opposites: 'In contrapposizione al personaggio di vittima si è delineato poi quello della donna che indaga, che ricostruisce i fatti, le cose, ci ragiona sopra' (*Conversazione con Dacia Maraini*, 30) [In contrast to the character of the victim there emerged the character of the woman who investigates, who reasons, who reconstructs the facts]. Despite the obvious differences between the two characters, Michela is struck by certain points of contact between the victim and herself. At first, her identification with Angela is an external one. Michela notes that the neighbours in the apartment building treated them equally, 'tutte e due eravamo "da proteggere" secondo la mentalità del palazzo, perché vivevamo sole' (*Voci*, 10) [According to our neighbors, both of us were in need of protection because we lived alone] (*Voices*, 4). But Michela quickly internalizes the perception and begins to identify with Angela Bari. As she contemplates the photograph of the victim splashed across the daily newspapers, she remarks: 'Mi sembra di conoscerla così bene, eppure non so niente di lei. E il fatto che sia stata così brutalmente straziata mi sembra improvvisamente una offesa fatta a me personalmente' (*Voci*, 30) [I seem to know her so well, yet I know nothing about her. And the fact that she has been so brutally torn apart suddenly seems like something that has been done to me] (*Voices*, 22).

Michela's identification with the murder victim becomes more and more insistent as the story unfolds. No sooner does the narrator observe that Angela opened the door to her assassin than she makes another startling observation: 'Quante volte ho aperto anch'io senza guardare, senza controllare, con l'impeto di un gesto di accoglienza felice!' (*Voci*, 123) [How many times have I also opened my door with an impulsive welcome without first looking or checking!] (*Voices*, 99–100). That Michela could inadvertently step into the role of the victim is suggested repeatedly throughout the novel. This is an interesting variation on an age-old formula of the *romanzo poliziesco*. The identification of the detective with the culprit is a cliché that dates back to Poe's Dupin and runs throughout classical detective fiction.[8] The relationship between Sherlock Holmes and Professor Moriarty is a case in point. The forces of good and evil, order and disorder, bear certain affinities that make them intellectual equals, worthy adversaries. In Maraini's *Voci*, this convention of the *doppelgänger* is present but in a new guise. It is the victim, rather than the killer, who becomes the detective's double.[9]

Michela's identification with the victim intensifies towards the end of the novel. Reading Joseph Conrad's *The Secret Sharer* in the wee hours of the morning as she battles her chronic insomnia, she has a revelation: 'Mi sembra di riconoscere nella doppiezza del capitano di Conrad qualcosa della mia doppiezza: non sarei tanto incuriosita da Angela Bari se non riconoscessi in lei parte delle mie perdizioni e dei miei disordini, delle mie paure e delle mie abiezioni' (*Voci*, 273) [In the experience of Conrad's captain, I seem to recognize something of my own. I would not be so curious about Angela Bari if I did not recognize in her some of my own loss and my own confusion, my fears and my lack of assertiveness] (*Voices*, 224). As Testaferri has pointed out, Michela recognizes her double as a result of reading Conrad: 'This indirect identification is pointing at a negative image of the double, that of Angela as victim' (47). What lies at the heart of the narrator's identification with the victim?

The answer to this question is slowly revealed in a series of repressed memories and flashbacks as the story unfolds. When Michela goes to Angela's mother's home to question her, she notices a photograph of Angela displayed on the piano.

> Quella bambina la conosco, mi dico, ma dove l'ho vista? E poi, frugando nella memoria, ritrovo un'altra fotografia del tutto simile, di una bambina con l'aria persa e il sorriso doloroso. La stessa fronte nuda e come indolenzita da un pensiero inesprimibile, gli stessi occhi che guardano il mondo con apprensione, la stessa bocca contratta che tende ad un sorriso pesto e propiziatorio, l'atteggiamento di chi chiede scusa di essere nata e spera, con la resa ai voleri altrui, di smontare il temibile congegno della seduzione e del possesso. Alla fine capisco: quella bambina sono io, in una fotografia fattami da mio padre. (*Voci*, 114)

> [I feel sure that I know that child, but where have I seen her? And then, searching through my memory, I remember another exactly similar photograph of a child with a sad smile and a look of being lost. The same forehead, naked and as if in pain from some inexpressible thought, the same eyes looking out on the world with apprehension, the same mouth set into a crushed, propitiatory smile: the attitude of someone who asks to be forgiven for being born and who hopes, by surrendering to other people's wishes, to demolish the fearful mechanism of seduction and possession. Eventually I understand: that child is me in a photograph taken by my father when I was just about the same age.] (*Voices*, 92)

The references to apprehension, to an inexpressible thought, to surrendering to other people's wishes, are gradually explained as Michela revisits memories and engages in imaginary conversations with her father. The most revealing is one in which young Michela and her father, stripped to their underwear, take an impromptu swim in the Arno. The father claims to have rescued the daughter from a strong current; the adult daughter of the dialogue questions the father's version of the story. The dream-memory ends where the father embraces Michela and explains: 'Comunque tremavi, tossivi, sputavi acqua ... ti ho stretto forte forte a me ... avrei dato la mia vita per te' (*Voci*, 171) [You were trembling and coughing and spitting up water ... I held you so close to me ... I would have given my life for you] (*Voices*, 141). The narrator never reflects further on this scene, nor does she ever explicitly connect it to the crime she is investigating. It is implied, however, that Michela's identification with Angela is grounded in a childhood seduction. It is equally clear that her identification with Angela is a function of gender – that all women can be called upon to act out the role of victim too often scripted by patriarchal society. It may be her very identification with the status of victim that allows Michela to solve the mystery.

Voci thwarts the reader's expectation of the Sherlock Holmes type of infallible detective and his less astute, Watson-like sidekick. Instead, we have a pair of investigators, one amateur and one professional, who each bring different insights and skills to the investigation. Where the characters differ most is in their *modus operandi*. While Adele has adopted a detached approach, distancing herself from the horror, Michela feels 'coinvolta' [involved]. At dinner with Michela, Adele Sòfia calmly peruses the gruesome files on recent unsolved crimes in Rome, while Michela is unable to eat. Each time she is faced with new files, new statistics, new cases, she is overcome by the gruesome nature of the crimes: 'la ripugnanza mi si annida in gola' (*Voci*, 34) [a feeling of repugnance lurks in my throat] (*Voices*, 25). At first it appears that this lack of detachment might hinder the investigation. But it might be argued that it is Michela's very passion, her feeling of involvement to the point of identification with the victim, that allows her to solve the crime. That Michela will be the one to solve the crime is foreshadowed by Avvocato Merli, who suggests that enigmas are solved through passion rather than through skill.

Michela exhibits her powers of 'ratiocination' in her reading of the fables taped by Angela Bari prior to her violent death. Each of the fables narrated by the victim features a tyrannical father who showers the daughter with gifts and simultaneously mistreats her. The twenty fables become progressively more ferocious, the final one ending with the daughter's violent death. When Michela follows this lead and visits the stepfather, she asks about the fables, 'che raccontano, ossessivamente, storie di padri, che vogliono mangiarsi le figlie' (*Voci*, 229) [which tell obsessively of fathers who want to devour their daughters]

68   The Novel as Investigation

(*Voices*, 189). The stepfather disavows any connection with the affectionate yet despotic father of the fables and identifies the character as Angela's real father, who died when the victim was eight years old. The narrator finds the stepfather's voice to be 'sincera e franca' [sincere and frank] as he makes his disavowal. As Michela leaves his home, however, she recognizes in the musical intonation of that voice 'una melodia interna che solo i grandi seduttori sanno produrre a volontà' (*Voci*, 230) [an internal melody that only the greatest seducers are able to put on at will] (*Voices*, 190). The tapes prove to be the most incriminating testimony in the case.

It is the amateur detective, Michela, not the professional Adele, who correctly reads the various clues in the Bari case. The fact that the competent, masterful inspector Adele Sòfia is on the wrong track much of the time undercuts Michela's initial impression of Adele as a symbolic mother. While Adele dismisses the Bari tapes as irrelevant, the narrator correctly reads the clues contained in the incriminating fables. Adele Sòfia is convinced of the pimp Nando Pepi's guilt, but he is ultimately cleared when it is found that his blood type does not match the sample discovered at the scene of the crime. The narrator continues to search for the identity of the assassin by focusing on a curious detail of the crime scene: the fact that the victim's clothing was painstakingly folded in an apparently habitual or ritual fashion. This detail later proves to be significant. With the incriminating 'evidence' of the fables in hand, Michela goes first to interview the stepfather and then to check out his seemingly airtight alibi. At the hospital she learns that there has been some confusion regarding dates. The stepfather was not, as was initially believed, in the delivery room the night of the murder but rather the night before. His alibi must therefore be discounted. Suddenly the detail of the folded clothes takes on new significance. The clothes are evidence of a quasi-incestuous liaison of long standing, beginning with Angela's abuse by her stepfather while still a dutiful child trained to fold her clothes neatly on a chair at bedtime.

The narrator's implied incestuous or quasi–incestuous relationship with her father gives her the necessary insight into the story of Angela's abusive relationship with her stepfather. The stories of Angela and Michela are variations on the theme of incestuous relationships that are at the heart of many of Maraini's texts, including the highly acclaimed *La lunga vita di Marianna Ucrìa*.[10]

The real culprit in both the Angela Bari case and all the unsolved crime files is patriarchal society itself. It is Adele Sòfia who, midway through the novel, inadvertently gives Michela the 'key' to the solution of the crime: 'Edipo cercava la soluzione delle miserie nei fatti esterni, mentre il male era dentro la sua città, dentro il suo stesso corpo, la sua stessa storia' (*Voci*, 132) [Oedipus was looking for an external solution to the misfortune he himself had brought upon his own city through his own flesh, his own history] (*Voices*, 108). Like Oedipus, Michela tries to understand what is happening as an external phenomenon. Only when she realizes to what extent Angela's death is caused by factors internal to the society in which she lived, indeed internal to her own personal history, will Michela have the answer to the riddle. But the solution to the Bari case will not answer the larger question of why violence against women has reached epidemic proportions. Throughout the novel Michela plays back the voices of the experts, sociologists and criminologists, she has taped in the course of her investigation. Some argue that rape and murder are 'intrinseci dell'ideologia paterna' (82) [intrinsic to patriarchal ideology], others maintain that rape is part of the preservation instinct of man ('istinto di conservazione'). Michela herself grapples with the issue of male aggression and violence against women as she replays the various experts who have testified on the matter.[11]

The conclusion of the classical detective novel depicts the triumph of 'ratiocination,' the apprehension and punishment of the culprit, and a society restored to the rule of law and order. In Maraini's novel, by contrast, these expectations are overturned. The professional investigator, Adele, suggests that tidy solutions are the stuff of detective fiction, not of real life. Despite Adele's admonition, the particular case in question is solved. Ratiocination triumphs to the degree that the guilty party is identified, both by Michela's 'intuitive' reading of Angela's incriminating fables and by Adele's more scientific methods, in this case the positive identification of the stepfather as the killer provided by the blood test. But the criminal commits suicide before he can be apprehended, thus depriving society and the reader of the retributive punishment that provides such reassuring closure in the classical *giallo*. More importantly, society is not restored to order. The identification of an individual culprit, in this case the stepfather, will do nothing to change the script of the victim written by patriarchal society. This explains why the author has stated: 'io non sapevo fino all'ultimo capitolo chi sarebbe stato l'assassino' (*Conversazione con Dacia Maraini*, 7) [I did not know until the final chapter who the murderer would be]. Any of the main characters who fall under suspicion could have been guilty of the crime, and indeed all were guilty of victimizing Angela Bari in some way.

Maraini is not the first detective writer to deliberately withhold the satisfaction provided by the sense of closure of the typical *giallo*. As Michael Holquist has pointed out, Borges, Robbe-Grillet, and other writers of metaphysical detective fiction have refused to assuage their 'deep sense of the chaos of the world ... by turning to the mechanical certainty, the hyperlogic of the classical detective story' (172). Maraini is not so much interested in undermining the syllogistic order implied by the classical detective novel as she is in undercutting the notion that the triumph of order in the solution of a single crime will restore order to society at large. Indeed, towards the end of her unofficial investigation Michela begins to recognize that the solution of the Bari case will provide a false sense of security. 'Appena si saprà chi è stato, nessuno se ne occuperà più, l'enigma sarà risolto e la sfinge resterà muta e inerte fino al prossimo "efferato delitto per mano di ignoti"' (*Voci*, 237) [as soon as the culprit is found, the mystery will be solved and the sphinx will remain dumb and motionless until the next 'savage crime by unknown hands'] (*Voices*, 195–6). Thus, when the Bari case is solved, the narrator is neither self-congratulatory nor jubilant. The solution of one crime among the mind-numbing number of murder cases, files, and mutilated corpses periodically inventoried throughout the novel offers little reason for jubilation. Indeed, in the final pages of *Voci* the question of guilt is reopened, as Adele Sòfia informs Michela that her own lover, Marco, is still a suspect and will have to submit to a blood test: 'Sembra impossibile liberarsi di questo delitto, perfino dopo una più che plateale e chiarissima soluzione ... la logica continua a chiedere sacrifici ... la sfinge sembra sorridere sorniona' (*Voci*, 300) [It does not seem possible to get away from this crime even after an obvious and patently clear solution. Reason demands sacrifices but for how long? There is a sly smile on the face of the sphinx] (*Voices*, 247). This open-ended conclusion thwarts the reader's expectations of closure and certainty. The author ultimately points the finger at patriarchal society itself. By withholding the reassurance afforded by the classical *romanzo poliziesco*, Maraini has written a compelling and thought-provoking exposé of one of contemporary society's least-well-kept secrets.

The open-ended conclusion of *Voci* includes the possibility that the narrator will write a book about the Angela Bari case as an exemplum of the rampant violence against women in patriarchal society. In the final chapter of the novel, after she informs Michela of the stepfather's suicide, Adele Sòfia suggests this course of action: 'Ah, lo sa che Cusumano ha rinunciato al programma in quaranta puntate sui crimini contro le donne? Ai proprietari della radio non è piaciuto ... sembra che l'argomento metta paura ... secondo me lei dovrebbe proprio farne un libro' (*Voci*, 300) [Oh, did you know that Cusamano has given up on those forty programmes about crimes against women? The owners didn't like it ... it seems the theme frightens people off ... I think you should make a book out of it] (*Voices*, 246–7). The reader does not know whether Michela will follow Adele's suggestion. The novel ends with a question: 'Uscire dalla malia delle voci, come dice Adele Sòfia, ed entrare nella logica geometrica dei segni scritti? Sarà un atto di saviezza o una scappatoia per eludere i corpi occhiuti e chiacchierini delle voci?' (*Voci*, 301) [Should I get away from the fascination of the voices to enter into the logical geometry of written signs? Would this be wise action or only a way of escaping from the sharp-eyed chattering bodies of the voices?] (*Voices*, 247–8). This conclusion functions as a kind of *mise en abîme*, a reference to the writing of the novel we have just finished reading. Although the fictional protagonist has not yet answered the question of the efficacy of writing, and has not yet committed herself to the project, Dacia Maraini on the contrary has decided in favour of the power of the pen. In conjunction with her 1985 *Isolina: La donna tagliata a pezzi* and her 1999 *Buio*, *Voci* gives voice to the victims of violence against women throughout history. Maraini exploits the conventions of detective fiction to shed light on the causes of the offence and to call for a remedy.

5 Ethics and Literature in *Sostiene Pereira: Una Testimonianza*

Antonio Tabucchi's 1994 *Sostiene Pereira: Una testimonianza* is a historical novel set in 1938 Lisbon at the height of the Salazar dictatorship. Tabucchi delves into Portugal's fascist past not only to shed light on that episode in history but also to comment on the present day. Like his 1997 *La testa perduta di Damasceno Monteiro*, the story of an episode of police brutality in contemporary Portugal, *Sostiene Pereira* is a cautionary tale of the need for constant vigilance in the unending struggle against oppression and abuse. Widely acclaimed upon its publication in 1994, the novel examines the gradual 'presa di coscienza' of a Portuguese journalist and the role that literature plays in the character's ethical formation. This chapter will examine how Tabucchi's novel addresses a series of questions regarding literature and its relation to ethics.[1] How does society assess the value of a literary work? What is the connection between reading and the lives of readers? Can the pen be used as a weapon in the struggle against injustice? As it addresses these questions, *Sostiene Pereira* argues for the importance of an ethically engaged literature.

Sostiene Pereira is a conversion narrative, the story of the aging Pereira's gradual awakening to the political realities of fascist Portugal. Pereira, once responsible for the crime pages for an important Portuguese daily, has become the editor of the cultural section of a Lisbon newspaper, *Lisboa*. As Jeannet has pointed out, Pereira is 'the Montalean type of literary man, middle aged, physically on the decline, and a lover of literature who aspires to remain aloof from history, particularly his country's disastrous political events' (160–1).[2] A chance event sets the character's conversion in motion. Pereira happens to read a philosophical reflection on death by a young man and subsequently contacts its author, Monteiro Rossi. He invites Rossi to collaborate with him on the cultural page of *Lisboa*. Specifically, the protagonist commissions Rossi to contribute advance obituaries of acclaimed writers in anticipation of their deaths. The meeting between Pereira and Monteiro Rossi proves to be a fateful one. Pereira's growing friendship with Rossi and his friend Marta becomes the catalyst in the aging widower's uneventful life, propelling him out of his lethargy and towards a reawakening.

Pereira is a monumentally uninformed journalist who gradually becomes aware of the extent of the fascist regime's crimes. This dawning awareness parallels a growing recognition of his responsibility as a journalist to expose those crimes. When Pereira asks a friend, the activist priest Padre Antonio, why the latter is so distraught, the priest replies, 'hanno massacrato un alentejano sulla sua carretta, ci sono scioperi ... ma in che mondo vivi, tu che lavori in un giornale?' (*Sostiene Pereira*, 15) [they've murdered a carter on his own cart in Alentejo, and there are workers on strike ... are you living in another world, and you working on a newspaper?] (*Pereira Declares*, 7). This encounter represents only the first of many episodes in which Pereira is reprimanded for his lack of awareness and reminded of his responsibility as a journalist. The waiter in Pereira's favourite cafe vents his frustration when Pereira asks for the latest news. The waiter replies in exasperation: 'Se non lo sa lei, dottor Pereira, che sta nel giornalismo' (*Sostiene Pereira*, 79) [If you don't know, Dr. Pereira, and you a journalist!] (*Pereira Declares*, 49). The resounding silence of the Portuguese press, which carries a front-page article on yachts in the New York Boat Harbor while suppressing the story of the socialist 'carrettiere' assassinated by the Guardia Nacional, slowly dawns upon Pereira. When he goes to visit a college friend both to escape from thoughts of 'il male del mondo' and to find a sympathetic ear, Pereira gives vent to his mounting concern and canvasses the state of affairs in Portugal: 'ci sono perquisizioni, censure, questo è uno stato autoritario' (*Sostiene Pereira*, 64) [they ransack people's houses, there's censorship, I tell you, this is an authoritarian state] (*Pereira Declares*, 40). Although his college friend disappoints Pereira by revealing his pro-fascist leanings, this encounter causes Pereira to recognize his anti-fascist beliefs and to articulate his own particular obligation as a journalist: 'Però io faccio il giornalista ... Allora devo essere libero, e informare la gente in maniera corretta' (*Sostiene Pereira*, 64) [But I'm a journalist ... So ... I must be free to keep people properly informed] (*Pereira Declares*, 40). The encounter

Ethics and Literature in *Sostiene Pereira* 75

with Senhora Delgado, a Jewish woman on the return train from Coimbra, functions as a further reminder to Pereira. Delgado, who is awaiting a visa to immigrate to America, notices that Pereira is reading a book by Thomas Mann, a writer who, as she points out, is not happy with the ominous turn of events in Germany. When Pereira concedes that perhaps he, too, is unhappy with events in Europe, Delgado exhorts Pereira to take action: 'Lei è un intellettuale, dica quello che sta succedendo in Europa, esprima il suo libero pensiero, insomma, faccia qualcosa' (*Sostiene Pereira,* 72) [you're an intellectual, tell people what's going on in Europe, tell them your own honest opinion, just get on and do something] (*Pereira Declares,* 45). The encounters with Monteiro Rossi, his friend Marta, the fascist sympathizer, and the anti-fascist Delgado gradually cause Pereira to re-examine his role in society as he takes on responsibility for the cultural pages of his small newspaper. In the final chapter, Pereira will rise to the challenge and use the power of the pen to expose the crimes of the Salazar regime.

Pereira is a gatekeeper-intellectual of sorts, deciding which writers will be eulogized in *Lisboa*, whose stories will be published in serialized form, which authors' stock will appreciate through mention in the *Ricorrenze* [Anniversaries] column. The protagonist's conversion is in large measure brought about through the process of appraising various European writers and their value to society. Pereira has a predilection for the French Catholic writers Mauriac, Bernanos, and Maritain. At his first encounter with Monteiro Rossi, Pereira suggests to the young man that he might provide an advance obituary of Mauriac. Rossi instead submits an unpublishable eulogy of Garcia Lorca, the Spanish poet and playwright whose anti-fascist activities led to his assassination by Francoist police in 1938 during the Spanish Civil War. The eulogy, as Pereira quickly points out, is unpublishable in the Portuguese press. Pereira continues to assign apparently politically 'safe' writers to Monteiro Rossi. Rossi unabashedly ignores Pereira's advice and instead provides eulogies denouncing proto-fascist writers like Marinetti and D'Annunzio or exalting revolutionary writer/martyrs like Mayakovsky. The writers singled out for praise by Monteiro Rossi include some of the self-same writers Tabucchi most admires. In *Sogni di sogni* Tabucchi imagines the dreams of twenty such writers, including both Garcia Lorca and Mayakovsky.[3]

In their unpublishable obituaries Monteiro Rossi and his friend Marta are practicing a form of 'ethical criticism.' Whether praising a literary work for its 'ethos ' or attacking it, the ethical critic draws a 'vital connection between literary experience and the lives of readers' (Booth, *Company*, 7). Rossi's obituary of Marinetti, the Italian Futurist poet, is an example of the practice of ethical criticism: 'Nemico della democrazia, bellicoso e bellicista ... Scrisse fra l'altro un manifesto ributtante: Guerra sola igiene del mondo ... Con lui scompare un losco personaggio' (*Sostiene Pereira*, 51) [An enemy of democracy, bellicose and militaristic ... Among his writing is another nauseating manifesto: *War: the World's Only Hygiene* ... With him dies a truly ugly customer, a warmonger] (*Pereira Declares*, 31). Rossi exposes the poet's bellicosity and denounces Marinetti as a writer whose work does society no good. Later, Gabriele D'Annunzio is included in the ranks of those whose work constitutes 'bad company.' Rossi concludes his D'Annunzio eulogy: 'Una vita non esemplare, un poeta altisonante, un uomo pieno di ombre e di compromessi. Una figura da non imitare, è per questo che lo ricordiamo' (*Sostiene Pereira*, 96) [A life far from exemplary, a poet high-sounding and grandiose, a man much tarnished and compromised] (*Pereira Declares*, 60). Rossi's singling out of the writers whose work he holds responsible for laying the foundation for the rise of fascism brings to the forefront the question of literature's relationship to and responsibility to society. Marinetti, the poet who exalts war in 'Zang Tumb Tumb,' an onomatopoetic description of a battlefield, is held responsible for how the poem may be used to glorify the brutal colonial campaign in Libya. Alternately labelled 'furfante,' [knave] and 'losco' [sinister], Marinetti is consigned by Marta to the list of writers whose demise would make the world a better place: 'ci sarebbero un sacco di scrittori che sarebbe l'ora che se ne andassero' (*Sostiene Pereira*, 29) [there must be dozens of writers who ought to be kicking the bucket] (*Pereira Declares*, 17). The denunciation of Marinetti and D'Annunzio is made not on the basis of aesthetic criteria. It is the clash between the underlying value commitments of the implied authors (Marinetti and D'Annunzio) and the readers, Monteiro Rossi and Marta, that produces their negative appraisal.

Pereira himself begins to follow the lead of Rossi and Marta. The moment in which Pereira not only embraces Rossi's appraisal of Marinetti but also accepts his own responsibility to give voice to that appraisal signals a decisive step in the character's awakening. As he takes his leave from his old college friend, Pereira remarks: 'Immagina che domani muoia Marinetti ... Marinetti è una carogna, ha cominciato col cantare la Guerra, ha fatto apologia delle carneficine, è un terrorista, ha salutato la marcia su Roma, Marinetti è una carogna e bisogna che io lo dica' (*Sostiene Pereira*, 65) [Imagine if Marinetti died tomorrow ... Marinetti is a swine, he started his career by singing the praises of war, he's set himself up as a champion of bloodshed, he's a terrorist, he hailed Mussolini's march on Rome, Marinetti is a swine and it's my duty to say so] (*Pereira Declares*, 40–1). This frank and candid appraisal, in which writers are held responsible for the effect their work may have on society, is one form of ethical criticism explored in the novel.

Tabucchi's *Sostiene Pereira: Una testimonianza* lays bare an age-old critical question, that of the value of literature to a particular reader and to a society. As Lawrence Buell has pointed out, there has been a revival of critical approaches that dwell on 'the moral thematics and underlying value commitments of literary texts and their implied authors' (7). Buell identifies some of the reasons for this revival, including an emerging ethical perspective within deconstruction and poststructuralism, particularly in the dialogue between Derrida and Levinas; a redirection of emphasis on the later works of Foucault; and 'the moral hazards of cognitive skepticism' (8). One of the critics cited as representative of the recent 'ethical turn' in literary criticism, Wayne C. Booth, reminds us: 'Of all the possible critical responses to poetry, the one with the most sustained written tradition is the question 'Will the experience of knowing this poem be good for me or my society?' (*Company*, 384).[4] It is precisely this question that is debated in *Sostiene Pereira*. Through Pereira's discussions and decisions concerning the value of particular writers, the author posits the validity of judging literature according to ethical criteria. The issue that plays out in these pages is not so much whether a particular set of writers should be extolled, emulated, or denounced. Rather, the novel, through the interplay between Rossi and Pereira and the foregrounding of Pereira's gatekeeper function, argues that it is legitimate to ask the question, What good will this book do me or my society?

Pereira's debates with Rossi regarding the value of particular writers of course do not take place in a vacuum. The context for their 'readings' of Marinetti, D'Annunzio, Mayakovsky, Gabriel Garcia Lorca, and a host of other writers is fascist Europe in the late 1930s. Clinging to the belief that he and his newspaper still enjoy freedom of the press, Pereira initially assures Rossi that he has complete control as editor of the cultural page. Yet Rossi's choice of authors to be eulogized forces Pereira to recognize the truth of the matter. Freedom of the press is an illusion: in order to preserve his job, Pereira must exercise self-censorship. Some writers are indeed too dangerous to endorse in fascist

Portugal. As Monteiro Rossi continues to submit his unpublishable eulogies extolling revolutionary writers and excoriating proto-fascist ones, Pereira repeatedly informs the reader that he should have thrown the eulogy away 'ma non lo cestinò.' The fact that Pereira keeps Rossi's subversive eulogies on file is an implicit acknowledgment of their worth. This recognition of the value of Rossi's writing is one of the important steps in the journalist's conversion. The relationship between the experienced journalist, Pereira, and the recent graduate, Monteiro Rossi, is one of mentor and student. Although Pereira initially plays the part of mentor, it gradually becomes apparent that their roles have been inverted: it is Pereira who ultimately comes to appreciate Monteiro Rossi's unpublishable eulogies and to learn from the younger man's unflinching candour.

What writers do constitute 'good company'? This is the subject of much debate in the novel. As Pereira acknowledges, his literary tastes differ substantially from Rossi's. While Rossi favours in his eulogies those writers whose revolutionary zeal is exemplary, Pereira prefers less political or politicized writers. He is a devout Catholic whose religious credentials are certified in his 'confession' to Padre Antonio: 'Io credo in Dio padre onnipotente ... osservo i comandamenti, cerco di non peccare' *Sostiene Pereira*, 144–5) [I believe in Almighty God, I receive the sacraments, I obey the Ten Commandments and try not to sin] (*Pereira Declares*, 91). He values the work of the French Catholic writers of the twenties and thirties, writers like Bernanos, Mauriac, and Maritain, inasmuch as their 'ethos' coincides with his own. Pereira repeatedly recommends to Monteiro Rossi that he dedicate a eulogy to Bernanos, the writer whose *Diary of a Country Priest* the journalist is in the process of translating for publication on the cultural page of *Lisboa*. Bernanos, an apparently apolitical writer who shares Pereira's religious and ethical values, would seem to be a 'safe' writer whose eulogy would cause the censors no problem. Yet it is ironically this 'safe' writer who, in 1938, published *A Diary of My Times*, inspired by his fury against Franco's atrocities in the Spanish Civil War. When Pereira learns from his friend the waiter that Bernanos has written a tract denouncing Franco and the Spanish Civil War, he takes immense pride in that fact: 'E un grande scrittore Cattolico ... lo sapevo che avrebbe preso posizione, ha un'etica di ferro' (*Sostiene Pereira*, 140) [He's a great Catholic writer ... I knew he'd take a stand, he's a man of the highest moral principles] (*Pereira Declares*, 89). Pereira has repeatedly informed Rossi of his lack of ideological commitment: 'a me non interessano né la causa repubblicana né la causa monarchica' (*Sostiene Pereira*, 86) [I am not interested either in the republican or in the monarchist cause] (*Pereira Declares*, 53). He is able to admire a writer's political commitment when it is based upon ethical criteria he shares. For Pereira, Bernanos's courageous 'prise de position,' based on a Judeo-Christian ethical/religious foundation, is more persuasive than an action based on a political ideology. Pereira's ultimate courageous act, the publication in *Lisboa* of an eye-witness account of Rossi's assassination by fascist henchmen, will be built upon the same ethical foundation that subtends Bernanos's denunciation of fascism.

The insistence on the need for ethics and on the contribution that literature can make to the ethical formation of the citizen runs throughout *Sostiene Pereira*. When Pereira comes to the full realization that his translation of Bernanos's *Diary of a Country Priest* will never be published in the cultural pages of *Lisboa*, he dreams of the possibility of publishing it in book form.

> Se non poteva pubblicarlo sul *Lisboa* pazienza, pensò, magari poteva pubblicarlo in volume, almeno i portoghesi avrebbero avuto un buon libro da leggere, un libro serio, etico, che trattava di problemi fondamentali, un libro che avrebbe fatto bene alla coscienza dei lettori, pensò Pereira. (*Sostiene Pereira*, 170)

> [If he couldn't publish it in the *Lisboa* well never mind, he thought, maybe he could publish it in book form, at least the Portuguese would then have one good book to read, a serious, moral book, one that dealt with fundamental problems, a book that would do a power of good to the consciences of its readers, thought Pereira.] (*Pereira Declares*, 114)

Pereira's dream of publishing a serious, ethical book is both a prescription for what literature might aspire to become and perhaps even a meta-fictional reference to the potential benefit of the book we are reading. Pereira posits not only the need for a particular kind of writing. He also posits the connection between the literary experience and the lives of readers. The beneficial effects of reading are summed up in Pereira's turn of phrase 'avrebbe fatto bene.'

Sostiene Pereira: Una testimonianza indeed emphasizes not only the importance of ethical writing but also the ethics of reading and listening.[5] The protagonist favours nineteenth-century French writers whose work apparently has no bearing on the political strife of Europe in the

1930s. While he resolutely tries to shut out the signs of 'il male del mondo' and seeks refuge in the work of Maupassant and Balzac, his moral uneasiness surfaces in his choice of text. The Balzac story 'Honorine,' whose translation he publishes in serial form on the pages of *Lisboa*, is a case in point. 'Honorine,' a story of repentance, reflects Pereira's state of mind and foreshadows the protagonist's own conversion. Furthermore, Pereira himself recognizes that the story might reach others and serve as a message in a bottle: 'Perché c'era da pentirsi di molte cose, e un racconto sul pentimento ci voleva, e questo era l'unico mezzo per comunicare un messaggio a qualcuno che volesse intenderlo' (*Sostiene Pereira*, 78) [Because there were so many things to repent of, he declares, and a story about repentance was certainly called for, and this was the only way he had of sending a message to someone ready and willing to receive it] (*Pereira Declares*, 48). Not only does the Balzac story have a bearing on Pereira's own conversion but, more importantly, the story is recognized as having the power to bring about in the reader a repentance and 'conversion' similar to that of Pereira.

The question of the power of the pen to speak to the reader in 'subversive' ways is dramatized in the discussion of the Alphonse Daudet story 'La Dernière Classe,' the story of a French teacher in an Alsatian school at the conclusion of the Franco-Prussian war. In Daudet's story, before the Germans occupy the village on the last day of class, the teacher writes 'Viva la Francia' on the blackboard as an act of resistance against the impending occupation. When his physician Dr. Cardoso questions Pereira about the wisdom of publishing translation of the Daudet story 'visto i tempi che corrono' [seeing the times we live in], Pereira claims that the story bears no relationship to 1930s Europe: 'Questo è un racconto dell'Ottocento, è acqua passata' (*Sostiene Pereira*, 129) [this is a nineteenth-century story, it's ancient history] (*Pereira Declares*, 81). Dr. Cardoso reads the hidden message in the story, the call to resistance by the Portuguese people, and recognizes the decision to publish the Daudet story as an important step in Pereira's conversion. Pereira's superior, the editor-in-chief, also easily decodes the hidden message: 'Un racconto dell'Ottocento, sì, continuò il direttore, ma parla sempre di una guerra contro la Germania e tu non puoi non sapere, Pereira, che la Germania è nostra alleata' (*Sostiene Pereira*, 168) [A nineteenth-century story it may be, continued the editor-in-chief, but it is nonetheless concerned with a war against Germany, and you cannot be ignorant of the fact, Pereira, that Germany is our ally]

(*Pereira Declares*, 109). The subversive power of the story escapes the ill-equipped censors of 1930s Portugal, just as the message contained in Vittorini's anti-fascist novel *Conversazione in Sicilia* escaped fascist censorship. However, the editor's anger with Pereira's decision to publish the Daudet translation and his insistence on Pereira's self-censoring such stories in future confirms the relevance of Daudet's story to events in 1930s Lisbon. This episode underscores the fact that it is particularly in authoritarian regimes that the subversive power of literature is recognized. One is reminded of the passage in Calvino's *Se una notte d'inverno un viaggiatore* in which the director of the archives of the police state recognizes the power of the written word.

> Nessuno tiene oggi in così alto valore la parola scritta quanto i regimi polizieschi ... Quale dato permette di distinguere le nazioni in cui la letteratura gode d'una vera considerazione, meglio delle somme stanziate per controllarla e reprimerla? Là dov'è oggetto di tali attenzioni, la letteratura acquista un'autorità straordinaria. (238–9)

> Nobody these days holds the written word in such high esteem as police states do ... What statistic allows one to identify the nations where literature enjoys true consideration better than the sums appropriated for controlling it and suppressing it? Where it is the object of such attentions, literature gains an extraordinary authority. (*If on a Winter's Night a Traveler*, 235–6).

As Calvino's character eloquently demonstrates, the full value of a literary work may paradoxically be proven at the moment when a society attempts to suppress it.

Pereira's conversion story is not recounted in the first-person, autobiographical mode. The protagonist is not the narrator, but the *focalisateur* whose experiences are recounted to the narrator for transcription. The title and subtitle of the novel, *Sostiene Pereira: Una testimonianza*, point to the dual nature of the narrative – Pereira is a witness whose testimony is recorded by a narrator/transcriber. The novel begins with the words 'Sostiene Pereira,' and the formula is repeated over ten times in the first chapter. This repeated, almost obsessive use of the formula continues throughout the novel. What is the significance of this device? Interpretations have varied widely. One reviewer, Coletti, argues that the repetition of the phrase begins by underscoring the questionable nature of the testimony but quickly becomes an affirmation of the veracity of Pereira's statements. Bernardelli argues that the obsessive use of the refrain 'sostiene Pereira' immediately conjures up the figure of an external narrator who casts in doubt the veracity or completeness of the narrative (3). Others find that the viewpoint offered to the reader by the use of this device is limited but not unreliable.[6]

A close reading of how the refrain 'sostiene Pereira' functions in the novel is revealing. There is no question that the information provided by the witness to the transcriber/narrator is limited. Throughout the novel, as Pereira testifies to events leading to the assassination of Monteiro Rossi, he hints at and simultaneously suppresses irrelevant details. These usually have to do with dreams, often of his youth and early married life. On his first day at the clinic, Pereira goes for a midday nap and reports: 'Fece un bel sogno, un sogno della sua giovinezza ... ma Pereira preferisce non dire come continuava, perché il suo sogno non ha niente a che vedere con questa storia, sostiene' (*Sostiene Pereira*, 108) [He dreamt a lovely dream, a dream of his youth ... But Pereira prefers not to say how it went on because his dream has nothing to do with these events, he declares] (*Pereira Declares*, 68). This passage is typical of the repeated withholding of information that both intrigues and frustrates the reader. Ultimately, however, Pereira's reticence adds psychological depth to the character and greater veracity to the story. Another interesting effect produced by the split narrative voice is the ironic distance between the witness and the transcriber. There are frequent passages in which Pereira claims not to understand the motives for his actions or thoughts. For example, as he gives shelter to Monteiro Rossi, now a fugitive from the law, Pereira testifies: 'Non so perché faccio tutto questo per lei' (*Sostiene Pereira*, 177) [I don't know why I'm doing all this for you] (*Pereira Declares*, 116). The narrator, and the reader, know that Pereira is assisting Monteiro Rossi for a host of reasons ranging from his paternal feelings towards the young man to his gradual awakening to the need for action. In this passage, as throughout the novel, the narrator and the reader are one step ahead of Pereira. The interplay between what Pereira wishes to tell and what he wishes to keep private, between what Pereira cannot understand even as the reader and narrator/transcriber gain insight into the character's motivations, ultimately lends credibility to Pereira's testimony.

Before whom is Pereira testifying? Some critics have read the 'sostiene Pereira' refrain in a judicial context. Klopp, for example, reads this phrase as alluding to a 'politically damning confession' provided to the fascist police under duress.[7] Jansen has pointed out that the words 'sostiene Pereira' 'clearly refer to a juridical political testimony but do not exclude other interpretations' (203). Tabucchi himself has endorsed one particular interpretation – Bertone's assertion that Pereira is testifying before 'il tribunale della letteratura.'[8] Whether we consider that Pereira is testifying before the fascist police, before the tribunal of literature, or before the tribunal of humanity itself,[9] one point is clear. The notion of testimony at play in *Sostiene Pereira: Una testimonianza* underscores the presence of an addressee and an obligation to that implied other. As Shoshana Felman has argued: 'To testify before a court of Law or before the court of history and of the future; to testify, likewise, before an audience of readers or spectators ... is more than simply to report a fact or an event ... Memory is conjured here essentially in order to address another, to impress upon a listener, to appeal to a community ... To testify is thus not merely to narrate but to commit oneself' (39). This same sense of commitment to a community of listeners is inherent in Pereira's act of testimony and causes the reader to pay heed to the protagonist's words.

Pereira's ultimate conversion is confirmed by the final act of the novel, the writing of the exact account of the assassination of Monteiro Rossi at the hands of the Salazar henchmen and the publication of that account in *Lisboa*. Pereira's eulogy of Monteiro Rossi, entitled 'Assassinato un giornalista,' begins by extolling Rossi's journalistic contributions: 'Ha scritto testi su grandi scrittori della nostra epoca, come Majakovskji, Marinetti, D'Annunzio, García Lorca' (*Sostiene Pereira*, 202) [He wrote texts on many great writers of our time, including Mayakovsky, Marinetti, D'Annunzio, García Lorca] (*Pereira Declares*, 132). After expressing his hope that these articles will someday be published, Pereira describes in unflinching terms the assassination of his young friend and names Rossi's assassins. Pereira's *J'accuse* points the finger at the two fascist henchmen Fonseca and Lima, as well as their commanding officer. The journalist systematically describes the circumstances surrounding Pereira's assassination by the fascist thugs and the brutality of their attack: 'Era stato pestato a sangue, e dei colpi, inferti con il manganello e con il calcio della pistola, gli avevano fracassato il cranio' (*Sostiene Pereira*, 203) [He had been beaten to a pulp, and the blows, inflicted with a cosh or the butt of a pistol, had smashed his skull] (*Pereira Declares*, 133). Pereira's narrative serves as a tribute to Rossi, a testimony to the crimes of the Salazar regime, and a demand for justice. The journalist signs the incriminating document and departs to submit it to the unsuspecting typesetter, duped into believing that the article has been pre-approved. Pereira is asked by the waiter at the Cafe Orchidea, where he stops for coffee before submitting the subversive article, whether the reports from Radio London are correct: 'Dicono che viviamo in una dittatura, ... e che la polizia tortura le persone ... Lei che ne dice, dottor Pereira?' (*Sostiene Pereira*, 204) [They said we're living under a dictatorship, and that the police are torturing people ... Well what do you say, Dr. Pereira?] (*Pereira Declares*, 134). Pereira unequivocally confirms the reports of the misdeeds of the Salazar regime and strengthens his resolve to bring these misdeeds to light. His courageous decision to publish his indictment of the fascist regime brings us back to the subtitle of the novel, *Una testimonianza*, and to the importance of using writing to bear witness. The obligation to take up the pen to bear witness to crimes against humanity, to point fingers and name names, is a subject that Tabucchi also treats in *La testa perduta di Damasceno Monteiro*. Like the protagonist of that novel Pereira understands the importance of the act of bearing witness, of naming names.

Sostiene Pereira: Una testimonianza is of course a work of fiction. Yet it is a fiction that cannot be dismissed as mere fantasy. Early in the novel the protagonist recalls a dictum often repeated by his uncle, a failed writer: 'La filosofia sembra che si occupi solo della verità, ma forse dice solo fantasie, e la letteratura sembra che si occupi solo di fantasie, ma forse dice la verità' (*Sostiene Pereira*, 30) [Philosophy appears to concern itself only with the truth, but perhaps expresses only fantasies, while literature appears to concern itself only with fantasies, but perhaps it expresses the truth] (*Pereira Declares*, 17–18). Here Tabucchi's novel self-consciously proclaims the authority of literature. *Sostiene Pereira: Una testimonianza* aspires to be the kind of book described by the failed writer. The novel captures many aspects of Portuguese society under the Salazar regime. As the author explains in the peritextual note, the name *Pereira* was borrowed from T.S. Eliot, while the character Pereira was inspired by a Portuguese journalist-in-exile with whom Tabucchi made a passing acquaintance in Paris in the 1960s.[10] The journalist went into exile after publishing, through a ruse similar to the one Pereira used in the novel, an article highly critical of the Salazar dictatorship. Why did the funeral of this casual acquaintance inspire in Tabucchi the need to create the fictional Pereira? The story of an introverted intellectual who gradually awakens to the fascist abuses surrounding him is not unrelated to the present day. Tabucchi clearly sees parallels between the Europe of 1938 and Europe in 1993, the year in which the author penned his novel. 'Ripensai all'Europa sull'orlo del disastro della seconda Guerra mondiale, alla Guerra civile spagnola, alle tragedie del nostro *passato prossimo*. E nell'estate del novantatré, quando Pereira, divenuto un mio vecchio amico, mi aveva raccontato la sua storia, io potei scriverla' (*Sostiene Pereira*, 213, my emphasis) [I thought about Europe on the brink of the disaster of the Second World War, about the Spanish Civil War, about the tragedies of our *recent past*. And in the summer of 1993 when Pereira, by now an old friend, told me his story, I was able to write it] (my translation). Tabucchi's insistence on the proximity of the fascist past reminds us that fascism is an ever-present threat. The author, who refers both in his interviews and in *La testa perduta di Damasceno Monteiro* to the recent Council of Europe report documenting torture and police brutality in so-called civilized states, is painfully aware that the injustices of 1930s Europe have not been eradicated.[11] *Sostiene Pereira: Una testimonianza* is informed by Tabucchi's sense of obligation as a writer to bear witness, albeit in a fictional mode, to crimes against humanity such as those documented in the Council of Europe report.

The ethical framework within which Pereira makes his courageous decision to denounce fascist crimes is not identical to the ethical compass guiding Antonio Tabucchi the writer. Indeed, as Tabucchi himself has acknowledged, one might legitimately ask, What is the ethical framework remaining to the postmodern writer or reader? In an interview with Carlos Gumpert in 1995, Tabucchi discusses postmodernity, the loss of faith in eighteenth-century rationalism, and his perception of the need for a 'rational literature' ('letteratura razionale') that seeks alternative modes of reason. The author makes a telling observation.

> Io sono un laico, non un cattolico. Tuttavia credo che esistano delle regole che bisogna rispettare e queste regole, in fondo, le ha inventate la religione, l'etica religiosa, basata sui dieci comandamenti, che sono stati il fondamento di tutte le etiche posteriori, perfino di quello a carattere laico ... Ad ogni modo, in un mondo così corrotto come il nostro, che sembra aver perduto ogni riferimento etico, dire rubare non è bene, non dico che sia il dovere di uno scrittore, ma nemmeno mi sembra eccessivo. (102–3)

> [I am secular, I am not a Catholic. Nonetheless I believe that there exist rules that must be obeyed. These rules have been invented by religion, religious ethics, based on the Ten Commandments. The Ten Command-

ments are at the basis of all subsequent ethical systems, even those of a secular nature ... In any case, in a world as corrupt as ours, a world which seems to have lost every ethical reference, to say stealing is not good, may not be the duty of the writer but it certainly does not seem to me to be excessive.

In a postmodern world often characterized by nihilism or moral relativism, the author acknowledges the need for ethics and underscores the ethical potential of writing. When asked whether he considers himself to be a 'moralista privo di morale,' a helpless witness to 'il male,' Tabucchi vigorously eschews this characterization and instead outlines an active and positive role for the writer: 'Io credo di non aver divorziato dal tempo in cui devo vivere: non so molto bene se io ne sia l'interprete o il testimone, ma in ogni caso, partecipo ad esso' (103) [I believe that I have not divorced myself from the times in which I live: I don't really know whether I am an interpreter or a witness but in any case I participate in the world]. Torn between the substantives 'interpreter' or 'witness' to describe his position as a writer, Tabucchi opts instead for the first-person verb 'partecipo,' and with that word rejects the option of abandonment or withdrawal from the world.[12] This participatory stance of the writer towards an unjust and intractable world is both defined and embraced in *Sostiene Pereira: Una testimonianza*. Tabucchi uses his novel to work through the nature of the relationship between writing and society in a particular historical context and to uphold the idea of the power of the pen.

6 Detection, Activism, and Writing in *La testa perduta di Damasceno Monteiro*

Like Leonardo Sciascia and Dacia Maraini, Antonio Tabucchi exploits the detective genre for a variety of purposes. In both *Nottorno indiano* (1984) and *Il filo dell'orizzone* (1986) he draws upon the conventions of the *romanzo poliziesco* while departing from the norms of the genre in important respects.[1] The author has frequently mentioned his predilection for detective novels, whether of the popular or the literary variety.[2] In his 1997 *La testa perduta di Damasceno Monteiro* Tabucchi draws upon the detective genre in order to expose injustice and denounce a social problem that knows no national boundaries. The novel is a cautionary tale of torture and police brutality in supposedly civilized states. At the same time it self-consciously explores the nature and value of writing itself. In this chapter I will trace the progress of the investigation into a crime that comes to symbolize a larger social ill while examining the way in which the status, limits, and utility of writing are explored. Like Tabucchi's 1984 *Sostiene Pereira*, *La testa perduta* is a powerful defense of the power of the pen to combat injustice.

La testa perduta di Damasceno Monteiro opens with the discovery of a corpse by a gypsy encamped on the outskirts of the Portuguese city of Oporto. The distinguishing feature of the corpse is that it is missing a head. This is not merely a macabre variation on the typical 'body in the library' conceit that serves to create interest and suspense in the classical or Golden Age *giallo*. As Tabucchi explains in his authorial note, the headless corpse was inspired by an actual event.

> Di reale c'è un episodio ben concreto che ha mosso la fantasia romanzesca: la notte del 7 maggio 1996, Carlos Rosa, cittadino portoghese, di anni 25, è stato ucciso in un commissariato della Guardia Nacional

Republicana di Sacavém, alla periferia di Lisbona, e il suo corpo è stato ritrovato in un parco pubblico, decapitato e con segni di sevizie. (*La testa perduta di Damasceno Monteiro*, 239)

[From actual fact [the author] has drawn one very tangible episode which set that imagination in motion: on the night of May 7, 1996, Carlos Rosa, twenty-five years old, a Portuguese citizen, was killed in a police station of the Republican National Guard at Sacavém on the outskirts of Lisbon, and his body was found in a public park, decapitated and showing evidence of torture.] (*The Missing Head of Damasceno Monteiro*, 185)

While the case remained unsolved for some time, Tabucchi attempted to solve the crime in his novel. Inspired by this 'fatto di cronaca,' he weaves a tale of police brutality and murder and of the two men who attempt to expose the guilty party. In keeping with the tradition of the classical *giallo*, the novel traces the movements not of the professionals, the police force charged to solve the crime, but of the amateur sleuths – in this case a young journalist, Firmino, who writes for the Lisbon daily newspaper *L'Acontecimento*, and a crusading lawyer, Mello Sequeiro, alias Loton.

Firmino is far from the superhuman mastermind of classical detective fiction. The investigation into the murder is slow and fitful. Progress is due more to chance than to the intellectual prowess of the sleuth.[3] While the classical *giallo* provides a preview of the detective's power of 'ratiocination' in the early pages of the novel, *La testa perduta* features a sleuth who has difficulty rising to a series of challenges. Firmino is disoriented in navigating the streets of the city of Oporto. When he interviews the gypsy who discovered the corpse, he has difficulty understanding the dialect spoken. The one piece of information he gleans from the gypsy is the logo on the victim's T-shirt, 'Stones of Portugal.' At first this leads to a dead end. Firmino visits a T-shirt shop, but the clerk cannot identify the logo on the shirt. The sleuth is disconcertingly unable to rise to the challenge of decoding the cipher. Only when Firmino receives an anonymous tip is he able to trace the shirt to a stone supplier, Stones of Portugal, and to solve the mystery of the victim's identity. He learns that, following a theft in the store, a young man by the name of Damasceno Monteiro has been missing for five days. The journalist's suspicion that the missing person and the headless cadaver are one and the same is confirmed when the victim's head is discovered in the Douro River and identified by Damasceno's mother.

In short, Firmino is depicted in the early chapters of the novel as a reluctant and rather mediocre sleuth. His talents seem to lie in another direction. His true vocation is literary criticism. From the moment he is introduced, the day he returns to his job at the newspaper following a brief vacation, Firmino is torn between his work as a journalist and his scholarly vocation. He looks longingly at the Biblioteca Nazionale, where he has pursued the initial stages of a research project. 'Pensò ai pomeriggi passati nella sala di lettura a studiare i romanzi di Vittorini e al suo vago progetto di scrivere un saggio che avrebbe intitolato *L'infiuenza di Vittorini sul romanzo portoghese del dopoguerra'* (*La testa perduta*, 22) [He thought of the afternoons spent in the reading room studying the novels of Elio Vittorini and his vague project of writing a critical essay to be called 'The Influence of Vittorini on the Post-War Portuguese Novel'] (*The Missing Head*, 10). Firmino's desire to pursue literary studies becomes a recurrent motif in the novel. As he arrives in Oporto to investigate the mystery of the headless corpse for his Lisbon newspaper, he indulges again in a fantasy of literary and academic glory: 'E pensò come sarebbe stato bello scrivere il suo libro su Vittorini e il romanzo portoghese del dopoguerra, era sicuro che avrebbe costituito un avvenimento nell'ambiente accademico, magari gil avrebbe perfino aperto il porto del dottorato di ricerca' (*La testa perduta*, 32) [He thought how wonderful it would be to write his book on Vittorini and the post-war Portuguese novel, he was sure it would be an event in the academic world, and might even lead eventually to a research grant] (*The Missing Head*, 18–19). Firmino's interest in the politically committed literature of the post-war period introduces the question of the utility of fiction and leads into a broader discussion of the value of literature that subtends the entire novel.

The question of 'whodunnt' is solved midway through the novel when the anonymous tipster requests a meeting with Firmino. The informant tells Firmino that a sergeant in the Guardia Nacional, Titanio Silva, the kingpin of drug distribution in Oporto, has been receiving shipments of heroin in the shipping crates received at Stones of Portugal. Damasceno Monteiro, a stock boy, was caught by Titanio Silva in the act of stealing four packets of heroin. The tipster, a friend of the victim and driver of the getaway car, informs the journalist that he witnessed the capture of Damasceno Monteiro by the Guardia Nacional. The vicious treatment of the victim by Titanio Silva, nicknamed 'Grillo Verde' [the Green Cricket], leaves little doubt in the eyes of the witness that the sergeant is the culprit. What remains to be discovered in the second half of the novel is not the identity of the guilty party, but whether the guilty will be punished, whether justice will ultimately prevail.

The long arm of the law is personified in the character of Mello Sequeiro, aka Loton. Loton, hired by the newspaper to assist the impoverished Monteiro family, is a crusading lawyer, a defender of the poor, the downtrodden, the *emarginati*. His work represents an attempt to make amends for the centuries of oppression and mistreatment of the poor by upper-class families like his own, 'una specie di correzione tardiva della Storia, un paradossale rovesciamento della coscienza di classe' (*La testa perduta*, 111) [a kind of tardy penitence for history, a paradoxical inversion of class consciousness] (*The Missing Head*, 81). Unlike Firmino, Loton conforms in many respects to the model of the classical detective. The Great Detective in the Dupin–Holmes tradition is a stock character exhibiting certain primary characteristics: 'They generally possess a physical appearance as distinctive as Holmes' hawklike profile – they may be either very tall or very short, very fat or very thin ... They are usually pronounced eccentrics ... Above all ... the sleuth is blessed with a penetrating observation, highly developed logical powers, wide knowledge' (Grella, 87).[4] Mello Sequeiro, nicknamed Loton because of his resemblance to Charles Laughton, is an obese, eccentric loner. He often ruminates on the case and reaches solutions from his armchair. His bursts of investigatory energy are followed by moments of boredom, depression, and ennui, the likes of which were first seen in the characters of Auguste Dupin and Sherlock Holmes. From the moment that Firmino goes to meet the obese lawyer in his shabby, genteel apartment, Loton begins to play the role of the learned, eccentric mastermind, while Firmino assumes the role of the less astute, Watson-like character.

In classical detective fiction, the sleuth frequently entertains his sidekick with fragments of esoteric information. Auguste Dupin, Sherlock Holmes, and Hercule Poirot are each characterized by a quasi-encyclopedic knowledge. In *La testa perduta di Damasceno Monteiro* Loton, like his predecessors, regales Firmino with information about philosophy of law, ethics, literary criticism, and psychoanalysis. As in the classical *giallo*, the Watson-like sidekick is a stand-in for the reader, who is in awe of the Great Detective and benefits from the sleuth's encyclopedic knowledge. The discussions between the two characters appear to be irrelevant to the case at hand but actually bear directly upon the events that are unfolding.

One of Loton's favourite topics of conversation is the subject of literature and literary criticism. When they first meet, Loton and Firmino discuss not the case at hand but rather Firmino's research interests. When Firmino explains that he has been particularly influenced by Lukács, Loton begins to grill the journalist about Lukács's work. He reminds Firmino that Lukács's *History and Class Consciousness*, published in 1923, was undoubtedly influenced by events unfolding in Europe at the time. Loton's comments serve to underscore the fact that Lukács's reflectionist theory of literature as a mirror, however complex and distorted, held up to the historical world may also apply to Lukács's own work and to literary criticism in general. Firmino explains that he is interested in using Lukács to shed light on Vittorini's influence on the second phase of Portuguese neo-realism. As a committed activist, Loton might be expected to applaud Firmino's interest in Marxist criticism and politically committed literature. On the contrary, Loton's bemused and somewhat patronizing attitude towards Firmino's project seems to call into question both the value of the kind of 'letteratura impegnata' that emerged in western Europe during the post-war period and the value of politically informed, Marxist literary criticism. Loton, however, is less interested in privileging one literary school or current over another than he is in encouraging Firmino to keep an open mind.

Some of the most engaging pages of *La testa perduta di Damasceno Mornteiro* are those in which Loton digresses from the case at hand to discuss literature with Firmino. Throughout the novel and the investigation, Loton attempts to expand Firmino's literary and critical horizons. In answer to Firmino's question, 'Ma lei in che cosa crede?' [But what do you believe in?] Loton launches into a discussion of his favorite poets and their works. He extols Holderlin's poetry and waxes eloquent on one of Louise Colet's few successful verses, a poem addressed to her lover Flaubert. He agrees with Sartre's reading of Flaubert in *L'idiot de la famille*. Loton scoffs at the tendency towards overspecialization in literary studies, leaving Firmino speechless before the question, 'Scusi, giovanotto, ... lei pretende di studiare la letteratura, di volere addirittura scrivere un saggio sulla letteratura, e mi confessa che non sa esprimersi su questo fatto fondamentale, se Flaubert capì o non capì il messaggio cifrato di Louise Colet?' (*La testa perduta*, 129) [I beg your pardon, young man ... but you claim to be studying literature, indeed that you intend to write a paper on literature, and you here own up to me that you can't say anything for sure on the fundamental question, whether Flaubert did or did not understand Louise Colet's coded message? (*The Missing Head*, 96–7). Firmino's feeble defence, questioning what Flaubert has to do with Portuguese literature in the 1950s, is summarily dismissed by Loton. The lawyer's response is to insist that in literature everything relates to everything else. The exchange between young Firmino and his mentor Loton reads almost like a nightmarish PhD qualifying exam. Firmino's tunnel vision in defining his research project is a parody of overly compartmentalized subspecialties in literary criticism.

Ultimately, Loton's entertaining and learned digressions add up to a blanket defence of literature of all kinds, from Flaubert's *Education sentimentale* to the 'romanzetti di cattivo gusto' of Flaubert's day, from the surrealists to Gide, from the post-war 'letteratura impegnata' on which Firmino conducts his research to the science fiction with which the journalist whiles away his leisure hours. The lawyer clearly identifies with Firmino's youthful enthusiasm for books and encourages him to pursue his ambitions in the field of literary criticism. His frequent challenges to the young man's research project are meant to stimulate rather than squelch the latter's enthusiasm. As Firmino leaves Oporto at the conclusion of their investigation, Loton urges him to go back to his fiancée, an archivist, and to his research on the post-war Portuguese novel. He suggests the question of censorship in literature as a possible new research project for Firmino. As Loton sends the young man off to Lisbon, he alludes longingly to the work of Firmino and his fiancée: 'Lavorare con i libri è un bel lavoro' (*La testa perduta*, 204) [Working with books is a wonderful way of life] (*The Missing Head*, 158). These informal conversations between Loton and his protégé add up to a defence of literature in its entirety.

The lengthy digressions are interspersed with the sleuths' attempts to build the case that might lead to punishment of Monteiro's murderer. Loton advises Firmino to interview first Torres, the anonymous informant and friend of the victim, and then Titanio Silva, the corrupt sergeant. Both interviews are reproduced verbatim as a chapter of the novel, giving the reader a sample of Firmino's journalistic flair. In the second interview, the alleged culprit Silva admits that Damasceno Monteiro was in the custody of the Guardia Nacional, but claims that the victim committed suicide while Silva and his colleagues were out of the interrogation room making coffee. He is hard pressed to explain why there are cigarette burns on the body of the victim. His contradictory testimony only further incriminates him. The scandal breaks, all of the newspapers pick up the story, and Titanio's involvement, as well as the corruption of the Guardia Nacional in post-Salazar Portugal, is exposed. It seems, in short, to be a victory for free press, as the owner of Firmino's boarding house, Dona Rosa, concludes: 'Per fortuna c'è la stampa' (*La testa perduta*, 182) [Thank God for the Press] (*The Missing Head*, 139). Firmino's journalistic skill, concerning which he is so apologetic throughout the investigation, is used effectively in the service of a just cause. It remains to be seen whether the revelations in Firmino's newspaper will lead to the punishment of the corrupt police sergeant.

The mounting evidence that the victim had been tortured prior to his assassination by Titanio Silva leads Loton to share with Firmino his thinking on the subject of ethics and human rights. In another highly relevant digression, Loton tells the journalist about two actual cases: Artur London, a Czechoslovakian dissident tortured by the communists, and about Henri Alleg, editor of the *Alger Républicain* from 1950 to 1955, accused by the French of pro-Algerian sympathies and tortured in Algiers to make him denounce other pro-Algerian partisans. As Loton points out to Firmino, and to the reader, one suffered at the hands of the communists, the other because he was communist. Loton, uninterested in the politics of the victims, denounces both incidents as barbaric. Both Alleg and London chose to write of their ordeals, London in *The Confession* and Alleg in *The Question*. The latter, published in France by Editions de Minuit in 1958, sold 150 thousand copies in two weeks before being confiscated and suppressed by the French government.[5] As Jean Paul Sartre wrote in the introduction to the English edition of *The Question*, 'Torture is neither civilian nor military, nor is it specifically French; it is a plague infecting our whole era. There are brutes East as well as West' (25–6). Sartre's moral outrage, captured in this compelling introduction, is in keeping with Loton's aversion for torture, and for those who would justify its use in the service of the 'right' cause. As Loton points out, torture cannot be justified by an ideology: 'La tortura è una responsabilità individuale, l'obbedienza a un ordine superiore non è tollerabile, troppa gente si è nascosta dietro questa miserabile giustificazione facendosene uno schermo legale, capisce?, si nascondono dietro la *Grundnorm*' (*La testa perduta*, 176) [Torture is an individual responsibility, to say you're obeying orders from above is inexcusable, too many people have used that shabby excuse to shield themselves by legal quibbles, do you follow me? They hide behind the *Grundnorm*] (*The Missing Head*, 135). Here Loton is referring to the theory of the *Grundnorm* of Austrian legal philosopher

94   The Novel as Investigation

Hans Kelsen. As Norberto Bobbio has pointed out, Kelsen's theory of the *Grundnorm* or *Norma Base* is an attempt to liberate the law from any ethical responsibility.[6] He regards the theory of the *Grundnorm* as a reprehensible excuse for crimes against humanity undertaken in the name of a 'civilized' state. Loton ponders and then leaves unanswered the question of whether torture can be eradicated, or whether it is an innate and ineradicable part of human nature.

It is significant that both London and Alleg, the two victims of torture cited by Loton, took up the pen to bear witness to their ordeals. Indeed, it is because they took up the pen that Loton tells their stories to Firmino. Loton confides to the journalist that he himself once had ambitions to write a treatise denouncing torture: 'Molti anni fa quando ero un giovane pieno di entusiasmo e quando credevo che scrivere servisse a qualcosa, mi ero messo in testa di scrivere sulla tortura' (*La testa perduta*, 176) [Many years ago, when I was young and full of enthusiasm, and still thought that writing served some purpose, it entered my head to write about torture] (*The Missing Head*, 135). Loton has abandoned his youthful ambition to wield the power of the pen in the fight against torture. He has not only chosen action over writing; he also questions the value of writing. Yet Loton's dismissal of writing in the passage cited above masks a deep-seated ambivalence. While he himself has chosen *praxis* over *poiesis*, he recognizes that both are necessary.[7] He concedes to Firmino: 'Non saprei dirle se sia più utile scrivere un trattato sull'agricoltura o rompere una zolla con la zappa' (*La testa perduta*, 178) [I couldn't say whether it's more useful to write a treatise on agriculture or to break up a clod of earth with a mattock] (*The Missing Head*, 136–7). Loton is unquestionably drawn to those who choose the path of writing, those who, like Alleg and London, successfully use the pen as a battle cry to all civilized people and nations to denounce torture.

Tabucchi himself has taken up his pen on more than one occasion to bear witness to injustice. Most recently, in his 1999 *Gli zingari e il Rinascimento: Vivere da Rom a Firenze*, Tabucchi provides an exposé of the conditions of the gypsies in Florence and their mistreatment by city authorities.[8] The author accompanies his friend Liuba, and the reader, through the Florentine gypsy camps Olmatello and Poderaccio, and reports on the deplorable sanitary conditions in the camps: lack of electricity and running water; open sewers, leading to the spread of infectious disease; substandard housing. He reminds his friend that these substandard encampments represent the gypsy 'elite' in relation to the *clandestini*, gypsies who have no publicly supported or sanctioned encampments whatsoever. As Tabucchi points out, these conditions have made it impossible for the gypsies to continue to engage in the craftmanship that has characterized their culture. He traces the cultural roots of the persecution of the gypsies to Renaissance Florence and quotes verbatim the 1547 Ban on Gypsies. He also reports on a family of gypsies he had befriended and the tragic saga of their treatment by city officials. *Gli zingari e il Rinascimento* systematically undercuts the picture-postcard view of Florence that Liuba, and the reader, would cling to and provides vivid details of the deplorable conditions in the gypsy camps. These conditions, as he points out, are in violation of European Union regulations.

Tabucchi was writing both his exposé on the gypsies and the novel *La testa perduta di Damasceno Monteiro* at approximately the same period in the latenineties. His long-standing familiarity with the gypsy life both in Portugal and in Italy inspired the opening scene of *La testa perduta*. The first character presented by the author is Manolo, the proud and aging gypsy who discovers Monteiro's corpse, and the character to whom the novel is dedicated. As Tabucchi explains in the authorial note appended to the novel, Manolo is a fictional character inspired by an 'entità collettiva.' Tabucchi's sympathetic and knowledgeable portrayal of Manolo includes a description of the squalor in which he lives and a lament on the gypsy's loss of livelihood and dignity:

> sì che era Rey, quando i gitani erano onorati, quando la sua gente percorreva liberamente le pianure dell'Andalusia, quando fabbricavano monili di rame che vendevano nei villaggi e il suo popolo vestiva di nero con nobili cappelli di feltro ... Quelli sì, erano i tempi del Rey. Ma ora? Ora che erano costretti a vagare ... ora che non c'era più possibilità di fabbricare monili e mantiglie, ora che dovevano arrangiarsi con piccoli furti e accattonaggio, che cazzo di Rey era lui, il Manolo? (*La testa perduta*, 12)

[To be sure he had once been El Rey, when the gypsies were honored, when his people freely roamed the plains of Andalusia, when they made copper trinkets to sell in the villages and dressed in black and wore fine felt hats ... Yes, those were the days of El Rey. But now? Now that they were forced to wander ... now that they no longer had any means of making trinkets and mantillas, now that they had to shift for themselves as best they could with begging and petty theft, what sort of a fucking king was he, Manolo the gypsy?] (*The Missing Head*, 2)

96 The Novel as Investigation

This poignant assessment of the gypsy's plight echoes Tabucchi's description of the Florentine gypsy encampments in *Gli zingari e il Rinascimento*. Manolo's fear of the authorities and his insistence on reporting the discovery of the corpse through intermediaries reflects the neglect and even persecution suffered by the gypsies at the hands of authorities throughout Europe. Manolo becomes a kind of Everyman, representing the 'emarginati,' the marginalized of all societies.[9] These are the victims whom Loton is called on to defend.

Although Loton implicitly defends the utility of social treatises such as those of Alleg and London (and by extension Tabucchi's reportage on the gypsies), Loton's battlefield lies in the courtroom. The trial of Titanio Silva is one battle in the war against police brutality, torture, and crimes against humanity. The case against Silva appears to be airtight. As Firmino bids farewell to Loton and prepares to return to Lisbon, Loton cautions the young journalist against unwarranted optimism: 'Non si faccia troppe illusion' (*La testa perduta*, 203) [Don't cherish too many hopes] (*The Missing Head*, 157). He reminds Firmino that the defendant will almost certainly be tried in a military court, even though the crimes of which he is accused have nothing to do with war, and that the military will protect their own. The key question is whether justice will be served. This question will be answered at the trial of Titanio Silva.

The trial testimony is narrated in a curious fashion. Firmino becomes the *focalisateur*, the eyes and ears through which the reader is informed about the proceedings. The reader learns of the legal proceedings only after the fact, as the journalist reviews his notes on the return train to Lisbon at the conclusion of the trial. Firmino is an oddly unreliable and distracted narrator: 'Di quello che seguì, Firmino riuscì a memorizzare solo qualche frase. Cercava di prestare tutta la sua attenzione possibile ma la sua mente, come priva di controllo, vagava' (*La testa perduta*, 210) [Of what followed Firmino only managed to memorize a phrase or two here and there. He tried to pay as much attention as he could, but his mind, as if out of control, wandered off on its own] (*The Missing Head*, 162). Firmino's account of the testimony is fragmented and incomplete. The defence attorney's case is reduced to a few phrases ('bronze medal for military valor,' 'devotion to the flag,' 'lofty patriotism') in defence of Silva's record scribbled in Firmino's notebook. Loton's closing argument, like the testimony in Silva's defence, is reported in a detached, fragmented manner. This time, rather than relying on his notebook, Firmino resorts to a tape recorder. The tape recorder with which he records Loton's argument only picks up fragments of Loton's utterance. The reader does not hear Firmino's immediate account of Loton's presentation of the case, but rather a delayed reaction as the journalist listens to the tape in the train's restaurant car. The faulty recording with numerous gaps begins with the words of the philosopher Mario Rossi: '[la] domanda che rivolgo prima di tutto a me stesso: cosa significa essere contro la morte?' (*La testa perduta* 213) [[the] question I address chiefly to myself: what does it mean to be against death?] (*The Missing Head*, 165)[10] Loton's conviction that to be against death is the basis of any humanistic ethic is communicated in half sentences accompanied by lengthy gaps. Firmino repeatedly turns the tape recorder off to comment on the proceedings for the benefit of an off-duty waiter with whom he has struck up a conversation. The tape recorder picks up loosely associated snippets, including references to the Holocaust and to the French surrealists' denunciation of police brutality. The fact that the phrases are garbled and the transitions unclear makes the occasional clear passage stand out with greater intensity. One fragment of the lawyer's closing argument draws attention to torture as a crime that knows no national boundaries and cites recent evidence of police brutality: 'leggendo il documento degli ispettori del Consiglio d'Europa per i diritti umani di Strasburgo incaricati di accertare le condizioni di detenzione di questi nostri cosiddetti paesi civili ... un documento agghiacciante sui luoghi di detenzione in Europa' (*La testa perduta*, 218) [reading the reports of the inspectors appointed by the Council of Europe for Human Rights relating to places of detention in our so-called civilized countries ... a blood-curdling document dealing with places of detention in Europe] (*The Missing Head*, 169). Here Loton refers to an actual Council of Europe report on police violence throughout the 'civilized' world. Antonio Tabucchi himself cites this report as one of the inspirations behind his novel in an interview with the *UNESCO Courier*. The author explains that, while he was initially interested in researching conditions in Portugal, he realized after studying the report that 'the situation is much the same everywhere else in Europe, including in countries which seem more democratic. But democracy isn't a state of perfection. It has to be improved, and that means constant vigilance.' *La testa perduta* was certainly informed by the author's reading of this report and by his heightened sense of the need for vigilance.[11]

The logic of the connection between Titanio Silva's crime and the larger picture, crimes against humanity in all nations and times, rings loud and clear despite the disjointed quality of the narrative. The lawyer portrays the police sergeant as an all-too-common example of the lack of juridical control and legal protection in police stations. To help him construct the case for Titanio Silva's guilt even if, as Silva testifies, Damasceno Monteiro had committed suicide, the lawyer cites the case of Jean Améry. (Améry, an Auschwitz survivor whose writing could not alleviate the despair he suffered after his internment and torture by the Gestapo, eventually committed suicide in 1978.) If, as seems unlikely, Monteiro had died a suicide and not directly at the hands of the police, his desperate act would nonetheless have been forced upon him, Loton argues, as a result of the torture he had endured. It is left to the reader to make the connection between Améry's suicide and the possible suicide of Damasceno Monteiro. The closing argument trails off inconclusively on the tape recording as Loton is heard repeating the word 'infamia.' Firmino assures the off-duty waiter of the power of the lawyer's closing argument, which has been completely lost on the tape recording. 'Le assicuro che questo momento nell'arringa era una cosa da far venire i brividi, avrei dovuto stenografarlo' (*La testa perduta*, 224) [I assure you that from here on the lawyer's speech was something to send shivers down your spine, I should have taken it down in shorthand] (*The Missing Head*, 173). The reader must take on blind faith the assurances of the lawyer's oratorical power.

Loton's closing argument far exceeds the facts of the case before the jury. Taking his departure from a humanistic ethic, the lawyer constructs a ringing indictment of torture, police brutality, state-sponsored murder, and the worst crimes against humanity perpetrated in our century.[12] Why does the author choose to narrate the account of the trial, and particularly the account of Loton's indictment of crimes against humanity, in this peculiarly fragmented, detached fashion? Perhaps the 'static' in the message reflects the author's fear that the message will fall on deaf ears, that civilized people and nations will continue to allow crimes against humanity to be perpetrated in their name. Perhaps, also, the garbled message reflects the author's misgivings about his own power to wield the pen as a sword.[13] Ultimately, however, the effect is to challenge the reader to fill in the gaps, to forge the connections, to engage actively in the indictment of this crime.[14]

Loton's passionate and eloquent denunciation of torture and police brutality is to no avail. The guilty party, and the corrupt system he represents, goes unpunished. The only thing that Firmino manages to record fully in the pages of his notebook is the defendant's woefully inadequate sentence: six months' suspension for Titanio Silva for negligence in the line of duty. The sentence represents a complete miscarriage of justice, an outcome that Loton had to some degree predicted in his parting conversation with Firmino. As in the detective fiction of Leonardo Sciascia, the author declines to supply the consolatory conclusion provided by the conventional detective story. Much like Sciascia's *Il giorno della civetta*, Tabucchi's novel deviates from the norms of the detective genre, inasmuch as guilt goes unrecognized and unpunished. While reason triumphs on the intellectual plane in that the author provides the solution of the crime, it fails on the ethical plane because the solution does not lead to the administration of justice. In this sense, Tabucchi's novel can be considered an anti-detective novel.[15]

It is interesting to contrast the outcome of the fictional trial with that of the actual event that inspired the book. In an interview by Asbel Lopez in the *UNESCO Courier,* Tabucchi explains that *La testa perduta di Damasceno Monteiro* first appeared when the actual crime was still unsolved. The author was highly criticized by the Portuguese press for his portrayal of police brutality, a portrayal dismissed as a fiction in today's progressive Portugal. After the publication of the book, however, the actual crime was solved; the killer, Sergeant Jose dos Santos, confessed and was sentenced to seventeen years in jail. The Portuguese press belatedly marvelled at the author's talent for prediction. Tabucchi, however, demurred: 'But I don't think I have any particular talent for prediction, because when you have three or four elements in hand, you don't have to be a genius to reach certain conclusions' (48). No God-like mastermind is required to discover the guilty party in a case that was, as Tabucchi points out, all too transparent. Although justice ultimately prevailed in the Portuguese police scandal, Tabucchi scrupulously avoids such a reassuring conclusion in his novel.

The defeat of justice in the penultimate chapter of the novel is, however, not Tabucchi's last word on the subject. The final chapter of *La testa perduta* tells of Firmino's return to Oporto six months after the conclusion of the Titanio Silva trial in response to a telegram from Loton. The lawyer is preparing to appeal the case on the strength of new testimony. It appears that there is an eyewitness, a transvestite named Wanda who maintains that she witnessed the torture and assassination of Monteiro by Titanio Silva. Loton asks Firmino to write up the eyewitness's testimony for his newspaper in order to rekindle interest in the story. The journalist, who has just been awarded a six-month scholarship to study in Paris, agrees to set aside his research for a few days to oblige Loton. This time, however, it is the younger man, Firmino, who cautions the mastermind/lawyer: 'a quella testimonianza non crederà nessuno' (*La testa perduta*, 238) [no one is going to believe that evidence] (*The Missing Head*, 184). Loton's final word on the subject, 'E' una persona' [she's a human being], argues not only for the credibility of his eyewitness but also for the dignity of humankind. Although the possibility that justice will be served is remote in this case, Loton's dedication to the cause and his unwillingness to concede defeat give an optimistic cast to the open-ended conclusion of Tabucchi's novel. It is not only Loton's continuing activism that offers the reader a glimmer of hope, but also Firmino's dedication to the study of literature in all its myriad forms. The benevolent approval with which Loton regards his protégé and his work reflects the author's sense that political activism and writing may be complementary activities, equally useful in combating 'i mali del mondo' and equally worthy of pursuit.

Conclusion

The authors analysed in the preceding chapters do not belong to a single literary school, nor have they generally been considered to be 'kindred spirits.' What makes the convergence, towards the end of the millennium, of key works by Sciascia, Maraini, and Tabucchi so striking is precisely the degree to which these writers and their works intersect from dramatically different directions.

Leonardo Sciascia is of that generation of Italian writers that came of age in the immediate post-war period in which neo-realism flourished. Sciascia never adhered to the neo-realist prescription of quasi-socialist realism, and he kept his distance from the subsequent experimentalism of the Gruppo '63. From his first book to his last, the author remained true to his literary project as outlined in *La Sicilia come metafora*: 'lo scrittore svela la verità decifrando la realtà' (87) [the writer uncovers the truth by deciphering reality].

Antonio Tabucchi is generally associated with Italian postmodernism, although he himself is somewhat wary of embracing this label.[1] Ceserani argues that Tabucchi's fiction exemplifies many features of postmodernism, including 'the themes of the double or ambiguous personality, ... the experience of despair and solitude ... the importance of dreams, childhood fixations, and all the obsessions of literature, the open-ended plot ... the problematization of points of view and narrative perspectives, the nostalgic evocation of certain periods in recent history'[2] (380). Much of Tabucchi's work leading up to *Sostiene Pereira* and *La testa perduta di Damasceno Monteiro* is characterized by oneiric and fantastic elements that are utterly lacking in Sciascia. Yet, despite their formal differences, much of Tabucchi's work, like Sciascia's, is informed by a predilection for investigation and by a conviction that the writer's 'capacità di indagine' is a positive force in society.[3]

Dacia Maraini, one of Italy's most prolific and enduring contemporary writers, has not typically been read in the company of Italian male writers. Maraini's works, both her fiction and her essays, have defined and redefined Italian women's writing of the post-war generation.[4] Many scholars who have studied Maraini have correctly focused on the author's exclusion from the canon. This exclusion, without question true for much of her career, has recently been addressed and considerably corrected by edited volumes, tributes, and literary prizes (the Premio Bagutta for *Bagheria* in 1990 and the Strega, Italy's most prestigious literary prize, for *Buio* in 1999).[5] What is striking in this context is the way in which Maraini's work can profitably be read not only from a feminist perspective, nor simply in the company of other women writers. It can and should also be read as part of a dialogue with some of contemporary Italy's most interesting and enduring male writers. The key issue here is not so much who are the 'canonical' writers, a question that will never be settled for all times, but will be provisionally answered by each subsequent generation of readers. The question, rather, is whose work speaks to and informs the work of other writers. I hope that this study has demonstrated that the 'conversation' between the investigative fictions of Sciascia, Maraini, and Tabucchi is well worth listening to.

The investigative fiction studied in the preceding chapters cannot be fully contained under the rubric of detective fiction. There is an almost insatiable demand for detective novels both in Italy and beyond. This demand is fuelled by a basic human need, what Maraini in *Voci* calls 'il bisogno tutto umano e tutto profondo di risolvere un enigma' (34) [the deep and altogether human need to resolve a riddle] (25). It is beyond the intentions and scope of this study to provide a complete overview of the detective novel in late-twentieth-century Italy. From Fruttero and Lucentini to Camillo Camilleri, Carlo Lucarelli, Loriano Machiavelli, Renato Oliveri, Marco Vichi, and Luciano de Angelis, contemporary Italian writers have exploited and continue to exploit the popularity of the detective genre for a variety of purposes. These novelists are known primarily for their formulaic detective fiction.[6] By contrast, Sciascia, Maraini, and Tabucchi are known for a wide range of highly original and provocative works that cannot be contained within a single genre. Even Leonardo Sciascia, who, of the writers examined in this volume, is the most closely associated with the detective genre, draws equally upon other genres like the *racconto-inchiesta*. More importantly, the investigative fiction of Sciascia, Maraini, and Tabucchi may be distinguished from the current spate of Italian detective novels by its lack of a sense of play characteristic of formulaic detective fiction. These three writers resort to the detective genre, to the historical novel, and to the *racconto-inchiesta* not for diversion or entertainment, but in deadly earnest.

Investigative novels as defined for the purposes of this study are characterized by certain family resemblances. They feature not only idealistic detectives but also crusading lawyers, judges, journalists, and writers. These *dramatis personae* are propelled by an investigative zeal that transcends the gratuitous showcasing of the detective's intellectual prowess. The protagonists employ their intellectual powers to shed light on pressing social ills in our present and to delve into the origins of these ills in the remote and recent past. Each of the texts highlighted in this study explicitly or implicitly recognizes the responsibility of the writer and of literature, and each of these texts rests on a belief in the power of the pen. In their detective fiction and in other 'investigative' fictions such as the historical novels studied herein, Sciascia, Maraini, and Tabucchi stake a solemn claim for literature's ethical responsibility. These writers explore the author's contribution to the formation of an ethical/moral vision without which the most intractable of society's problems cannot be successfully addressed. The meta-narrative elements that this volume has uncovered in the works under review cannot be equated with the kind of navel-gazing, the playful *mise-en-abîme*, typical of certain postmodern works. The self-reflexivity studied in this volume is one that uses fiction to ask the question: What can the writer contribute to society through storytelling?

The focus on key investigative fictions of three of Italy's most prominent late-twentieth-century writers is not meant to suggest that these authors constitute a closed circle. Another example of an Italian writer whose self-conscious, investigative fiction bears many similarities to the works studied in this volume is Sebastiano Vassalli. Vassalli began his literary career as an adherent of the sixties experimental literary movement Gruppo 63. After breaking with the group and denouncing their poetics, he proceeded in the 1970s to produce three works, *L'arrivo della lozione* (1976), *Abitare il vento* (1980), and *Mareblù* (1982), in which he 'explores the ideological and social make up of Italy in the late 1970s and early 1980s' (Baranski, 249). Most recently, Vassalli has broadened his focus to include not only concerns with contemporary

Italian social issues but also attention to the roots of Italy's present in the more remote past. His 1990 *La chimera* provides a meticulous account of the life and death of an orphan girl accused of witchcraft and condemned to death in 1610 in northern Italy. He not only reconstructs from forgotten archives the story of the victim's persecution, but also identifies this operation of historical reconstruction as providing 'le chiavi del presente' (*La chimera*, 6) [the keys to the present]. As Zygmunt Baranski has pointed out, Vassalli's commitment to 'literature's inescapable social responsibilities' is a rarity in the fiction of the 1980s and 1990s.[7] It is precisely this uncommon and insistent commitment that I have underscored in the novelists under review.

There is a keen sense of urgency in the works studied in this volume. As Sciascia was approaching his death and Maraini and Tabucchi were approaching the end of the millennium, little progress had been made in addressing the ills that have plagued the twentieth century. The 'mali del mondo' chronicled in the pages of the novels under reabating. The investigative fiction analysed in this volume raises issues that, unfortunately, have only become more pressing at our present moment. At the beginning of the new millennium, one need only open a newspaper in any city in Italy, in the rest of Europe, or in North America to confirm that violence against women takes many forms but continues unchecked. The death penalty against which Sciascia lobbied so actively and to which he dedicates some of his most eloquent pages shows no sign of disappearing. Abuse of power is not a historical remnant of fascism but an ever-present reality.

When I began this project at the American Academy in Rome in the spring of 2004, the subject of torture, to which Tabucchi's *La testa perduta di Damasceno Monteiro* draws the attention of the reader, was not uppermost in my mind. Tabucchi's references to the Council of Europe report on the conditions of prisoners in places of detention throughout Europe, while disturbing, could be held at arm's length. I was shocked when opening the newspapers (both Italian and English-language papers being readily available in the coffee bar of the Academy) to find the sickening images of smiling American soldiers torturing Iraqi prisioners in Abu Ghraib. As the news continued to break over the ensuing days, as the images of American soldiers humiliating, sexually abusing, and torturing naked Iraqi soldiers made front-page news in Italy and throughout the world, the need for constant vigilance against the worst human rights abuses became painfully clear.[8] The denials of wrongdoing by both the perpetrators and their superior officers, the

Conclusion

attempt to lay the blame at another's doorstep, made the discussion of Kelsen's *Grundnorm* in *La testa perduta di Damasceno Monteiro* painfully relevant. The world has now discovered that the cause for concern about human rights violations indeed extends to 'so-called civilized states.'

There is one question that this study leaves unanswered – the question of the efficacy and limits of the sort of investigative fiction under review. This is ultimately a question that will be answered outside the realm of literary criticism. Whether these texts will make a difference to society will be answered by the readers of the novels in question. It can only be hoped that the reading of works such as *Porte aperte, Il cavaliere e la morte, Isolina, Voci, Sostiene Pereira,* and *La testa perduta di Damasceno Monteiro* will become part of the ethical framework informing the beliefs and decisions of readers.

Notes

Introduction

1 See Cannon, 'The Detective Fiction of Leonardo Sciascia,' for an analysis of Sciascia's first three detective novels.
2 See Cannon, '*Todo modo* and the Enlightened Hero of Leonardo Sciascia,' 282–91, for an analysis of this novel.
3 See Farrell, 147, for further discussion of Sciascia's return to fiction at the end of his career.
4 In *Leonardo Sciascia* Joseph Farrell provides an excellent comprehensive overview of Sciascia's work. See also Ambroise, *Invito alla lettura di Sciascia*, as well as the introductory essays to Ambroise's three-volume collection of Sciascia's *Opere*.
5 See Diaconescu-Blumenfeld and Testaferri, 4–7, for a detailed account of Maraini's literary career and extraliterary activities. Maraini founded the experimental feminist theatre company Il Porcospino in 1967. She participated in the campaign to legalize abortion in Italy in the 1970s and, more recently, she has joined activist groups in their campaign for the rights of Bosnian rape victims. She has conducted research on mental illness and investigated conditions in women's prisons throughout Italy, publishing her findings in Italian newspapers and magazines, including *Paese sera*, *Il corriere della sera*, *Il messaggero*, *L'Espresso*, and *L'Unità*. She has for years been engaged in research on violence against women. In a review of *Voci* for *La Stampa*, Maraini refers to her ongoing investigations as the inspiration behind her novel: 'Sono alcuni anni che raccolgo volumi, riviste, sulla violenza nei confronti delle donne; tre scaffali della mia libreria si sono ormai riempiti. La cosa che mi stupisce è che in Italia non esiste alcun genere di letteratura scientifica sull'argomento' (Ventavoli, 20). Maraini's

sociological investigations have frequently served as inspiration for her fiction. Her visits to female prisons throughout Italy inspired her 1973 *Memorie di una ladra*. More recently, her research on violence against women has informed *Isolina* and *Buio* as well as *Voci*. As Giovanna Bellesia has pointed out, many of Maraini's works deal with some form of violence against women, from domestic violence to rape to murder. In 'Variations on a Theme' Bellesia traces the theme of violence against women from *Donne in Guerra* (1975) to *Voci* (1994). She sees a subtle shift in the works from the seventies through the eighties to the nineties: 'In the long fight to stop violence against women, Dacia Maraini's outcry of the seventies has, in the eighties, found an outlet in her search for its roots. The nineties seem to be for her a time of further reflection on the causes of this phenomenon' (128).

6 For a complete overview of Maraini's work to date, see Diaconescu-Blumenfeld and Testaferri, eds., *The Pleasure of Writing: Critical Essays on Dacia Maraini*. Each chapter contains a useful bibliography on specific aspects of Maraini's work.

7 For a detailed analysis of Tabucchi's major works from his first novel, *Piazza d'Italia*, to *La testa perduta di Damasceno Monteiro*, see Brizio-Skov, *Antonio Tabucchi: Navigazioni in un arcipelago narrativo*.

8 Like Elsa Morante's critically acclaimed *La storia*, published the same year as Tabucchi's first novel, *Piazza d'Italia* rewrites 'official' history and becomes a kind of mico-history of Italy's vanquished and oppressed.

9 Francese provides a valuable and detailed analysis of Tabucchi's fiction in the context of postmodernism.

10 Ferraro uses the term 'impegno civile' to describe Tabucchi's *Sostiene Pereira* (157). Tiziana Arvigo also considers *Sostiene Pereira* and *La testa perduta di Damasceno Monteiro* to represent a turning point in Tabucchi's career. She identifies these works, as opposed to Tabucchi's earlier novels, as 'le opere ... di una "svolta civile"' (395).

11 See Coletti, 10, for this view of Tabucchi's 1994 novel.

12 See Wright, 78, for Maraini's detailed outline of her creative process.

13 If a work from which I quote has been translated into English, I cite from the English translation and refer the reader to the title and page number in that edition, which is included in the bibliography. If the work has not been translated into English, I provide my own translation.

14 The volume grew from a brief article in which Tabucchi takes issue with Umberto Eco's definition of the role of the intellectual, given in the latter's 'Il primo dovere degli intellettuali.'

15 In 'Storia e microstoria in *Piazza d'Italia*' (in *Antonio Tabucchi*) Brizio-Skov situates Tabucchi's first novel, *Piazza d'Italia* (1975), in the context of a histo-

riography of the period in which the novel emerged. Citing the work of Carlo Ginzburg, the author suggests that Tabucchi drew the inspiration for his first novel from the micro-histories of Ginzburg and his followers. Brizio-Skov persuasively argues that the strategies used by the micro-historian merge with those of the novelist. As the author maintains, *Piazza d'Italia* is in effect 'uno dei tanti possibili testi di Storia italiana' (32). The characters of the peasant, sub-proletarian world of *Piazza d'Italia* are repositories of a collective memory that is not the 'storia ufficiale' but the history of the vanquished'

16 See Claude Ambroise, '14 domande a Leonardo Sciascia' (interview), in *Opere*, vol. 1. Each of the three volumes of Sciascia's collected works is accompanied by introductory essays by Claude Ambroise. In addition to the interview, volume 1 includes Ambroise's 'Verità e scrittura.' The second volume of Sciascia's *Opere* contains the Ambroise essay 'Polemos,' and the third volume is prefaced by the essay 'Inquisire/non inquisire.'

17 As Adamo suggests, 'l'investigazione del passato non ha alle spalle il richiamo nostalgico di uomini e cose che furono: ma esprime l'esigenza di una 'lettura' attenta del presente (impossibile a farsi, senza cognizione alcuna dell'alfabeto di base, degli elementi di quella *storia di lunga durata* di cui parlava F. Braudel)' (133–4).

18 As Ambroise has pointed out in the introduction to the third and final volume of Sciascia's *Opere* (xlii), the death penalty is not only a recurring theme for Sciascia the writer; it is also an issue of continuing concern to Sciascia the citizen. The author's opposition to the death penalty motivated him to participate in an international symposium on the issue in Siena in 1987 and to write a review article of a reprint of the French translation of Beccaria's *Dei delitti e delle pene* for *Tuttolibri* (19 March 1988).

19 As Brizio-Skov has pointed out, it would be mistaken to assume that Pereira is testifying about a remote past: 'il suo messaggio, le sue verità risiedono in un intertesto che è la Storia, e la Storia, in senso crociano è sempre contemporanea. La crisi di Pereira segnala una crisi di valori non estranea alla nostra epoca' (*Antonio Tabucchi*, 6148).

20 See *Conversazione con Dacia Maraini: Il piacere di scrivere*, 31.

21 The importance of excavating the sites of women's history and memory was underscored by the author in the 1987 *La bionda, la bruna e l'asino: Con gli occhi di oggi sugli anni settanta e ottanta*. Dacia Maraini writes: 'What, exactly, is this difficulty in historicizing that is typical of women, forced to inhabit the margins of history? Or is this difficulty actually a refusal to link the past with the present? To give a meaning to things? To believe in what we have accomplished together? ... Women's memory is not preserved, not

valued. It is careless with itself to the point of dispersion. It grinds up, gathers, and then throws it all to the wind. In order to remember we must love our past, and therefore, in some sense, ourselves ... Female memory is wounded, deformed. It prefers not to look back to the past; like Lot, it fears being transformed into a pillar of salt' (248–9).
22 See John Grimond, 'Italy: The Odd Country, *The Economist*, 26 May 1990, 3–15, for a detailed analysis of the Italian political scene in the 1980s.
23 As quoted in *The Economist*, 20 February 1993, 45.
24 See Agnew, 106, for an informative discussion of the rapidly changing Italian political landscape of the late eighties and early nineties.
25 See Pertile, 16–17.
26 Jennifer Burns has suggested that the last decade of the twentieth century is a moment of acute constitutional crisis equivalent to the rise of the first Italian republic in the aftermath of the Second World War. In this climate she traces 'fragments of *impegno*' in the works of a wide range of contemporary Italian writers.
27 The term *impegno* or *letteratura impegnata* was exhaustively debated and defined by a number of post-war Italian writers and critics, including Vittorini, Calvino, Pasolini, and Asor Rosa. In her interesting recent study, Jennifer Burns argues against the notion that *impegno* simply faded away with the advent of *sperimentalismo* and the Gruppo 63. Burns distinguishes between the early, 'dogmatic' use of the term *impegno* and a later, more expansive understanding of the term. She makes an interesting case that the earlier theorizers of *impegno*, Vittorni, Calvinio, and Pasolini, gradually make space for an expanded notion of the concept that 'demands of the individual writer a serious moral, intellectual and aesthetic dimension' (37). She identifies 'fragments' of *impegno* in writers as varied as Pier Vittorio Tondelli, Andrea De Carlo, Silvia Ballestra, and Antonio Tabucchi. I prefer to reserve the term *impegno* for the neo-realist literature of the immediate post-war period and to find new terms, such as 'ethical commitment,' to describe the new departures of writers like Sciascia, Tabucchi, and Maraini. It should be added that both Tabucchi and Sciascia distanced themselves from the notion of *impegno*. In *La gastrite di Platone* Tabucchi characterizes *impegnato* as follows: 'Termine assolutamente innoportuno, che io non ho mai utilizzato, e che in Italia provoca disgusto immediato' (52). Sciascia implicitly distances himself from the notion of *impegno* in *La Sicilia come metafora* when he refuses to identify himself as an *intellettuale organico*. See also Sciascia's introduction to *Le parrocchie di Regalpetra*.
28 In the introduction to *Il sentiero dei nidi di ragno* Calvino describes the optimism of the young neorealist writers: 'Avevamo vissuto la Guerra, e noi

più giovani ... non ce ne sentivamo schiacciati, vinti, "bruciati" ma vincitori, spinto dalla carica propulsiva della battaglia appena conclusa ... Non era facile ottimismo, però, o gratuita euforia ...' (17).

29 In an interview by Carlos Gumpert Melgosa in the early 1990s, Tabucchi again paid tribute to Sciascia: 'Negli anni in cui Sciascia scriveva i propri romanzi sulla mafia, c'erano dozzine di sociologi, politologi e tuttologi che si occupavano dello stesso argomento ... Nessuno come lui ha saputo, tuttavia, captare tale fenomeno nella sua essenza con ugual verità e profondità' (105). The interview was published first in Portuguese, then in Spanish, and finally in Italian as part of Cattaruzza's volume on Tabucchi.

30 See Dacia Maraini's review of *La strega e il capitano*, entitled 'Un giorno Sciascia entrò nella città delle donne,' in which she writes: 'Un libro mi ha sorpreso più di altri, fra quelli di Sciascia, *La strega e il capitano* ... perché ha ritrovato e fatto sue, dopo solitarie elaborazioni personali, alcune delle idee che da anni le donne, a gruppi o da sole, portano avanti.'

31 See 'Premessa di Dacia Maraini,' in Cattaruzza.

32 In 1999 a special issue of *PMLA* entitled 'Ethics and Literary Study' featured an extremely useful overview of this 'ethical turn' by Lawrence Buell. Buell traced the reasons for the revival of an ethical or 'social value-oriented' approach to literary studies to a number of factors. These include the disillusionment with elements of deconstruction occasioned by the 'fall' of De Mann, the dialogue between Derrida and Levinas towards the end of Levinas's life, and the redirection of emphasis in Foucault's late work. As Buell points out, Foucault (particularly in *Ethics: Subjectivity and Truth*) 'anticipates – and probably has encouraged–later writers' propensities for deploying a critical vocabulary of "ethics" in rivalry to "politics" as a way of theorizing principled social engagement' (10).

1. The Power of the Pen in Leonardo Sciascia's *Porte Aperte*

1 For an analysis of the relationship between Manzoni's *Storia della colonna infame* and Sciascia's *Morte dell'Inquisitore*, see Cannon, *Postmodern Italian Fiction*, 40–59.

2 See Mullen for a perceptive analysis of Sciascia's historical *inchieste*. As Mullen has pointed out, 'the nature of [Sciascia's] relationship to history is illuminated by the different moments he repeatedly focuses on. These are: the Inquisition, the Risorgimento, the years of fascism, and his own contemporary society' (1).

3 In the history of Italian literature, the birth of the novel with Manzoni's *I promessi sposi* is synonymous with the birth of the historical novel. As

Ragusa has pointed out, Manzoni's novel is informed by the author's conviction of literature's ethical function.
4 All page references to Sciascia's work in this text are to the three-volume *Opere* edited by Claude Ambroise.
5 As Farrell has pointed out, these words had already been quoted by Sciascia in the pamphlet *La sentenza memorabile*, dedicated to the Martin Guerre case. See also Onofri for discussion of Sciascia's use of the Montaigne quote 'Leggiamo il passo in cui il narratore, sul filo dei divaganti pensieri del giudice, ricorda, senza citare la fonte, la frase di Montaigne che avevamo trovato nella *Sentenza memorabile*, ove si ironizza con quelli che danno un bel peso alle proprie opinioni' (266).
6 See *Opere*, 2:669–70, as quoted in Farrell, 156.
7 See Waldenfels's 'Levinas and the Face of the Other' for a clear and comprehensive examination of Levinas's concepts of *autrui* and *face*. See also Critchley's introduction to the *Cambridge Companion to Levinas* (ed. Critchley and Bernasconi) for an overview of Levinas's thought.
8 This is the same distinction Sciascia makes when he discusses in *Nero su nero* the appropriate motivation of the writer: 'dovrebbe sempre poter dire che la politica di cui si occupa è etica. Sarebbe bello che potessero dirlo tutti. Ma che almeno lo dicano gli scrittori' (*Opere*, 2:668) [he should always be able to say that the kind of politics in which he is interested constitutes ethics. It would be nice if everyone could say that. But at least writers ought to be able to say that.]
9 'Qual può essere il diritto che si attribuiscono gli uomini di trucidare i lor simili? ... Chi è mai colui che abbia voluto lasciare ad altri uomini l'arbitrio di ucciderlo? Come mai nel minimo sacrificio della libertà di ciascuno vi può essere quello del massimo fra tutti i beni, la vita? ... Non è dunque la pena di morte un diritto, mentre ho dimostrato che tale essere non può, ma è una guerra della nazione con un cittadino' (as quoted in Romagnoli).
10 See Booth, *The Rhetoric of Fiction*, for a detailed discussion of the concept of the dramatized narrator in literary history.
11 In his diary *Nero su nero* Sciascia comments on the perspicacity of the French in reading Italian culture. Stendhal comes to symbolize the paradoxical combination of keen understanding and misreading of things Italian: 'sempre i francesi italianizzanti hanno visto, in linea stendhaliana, splendere da noi quelle cose che a noi erano grevi ed oscure. Da Stendhal a Sartre (802) [always the italophile French have, with Stendhal, seen shining *chez nous* those things which appeared heavy and dark to us. From Stendhal to Sartre]. See also Sciascia's 'In margine a Stendhal' in *Cruciverba*, in which he

traces the various readings of Stendhal from Croce and Tomasi di Lampedusa to Gide, Gramsci, and Valéry.

12 For a discussion of the centrality of *Le parrocchie di Regalpetra*, see Ambroise, 'Verità e scrittura,' in *Opere*, 1:xxviii. As Ambroise suggests, 'l'unicità del libro [*Le parrocchie di Regalpetra*] sta probabilmente nella sua funzione di origine, di decollo di tutta l'opera.'

13 In his introduction to the third and final volume of Sciasca's complete works, Ambroise cites Sciascia's tribute to his young professor, Giuseppe Granate, who initiated him into the pleasure of reading, from the Enlightenment writers to the American writers of the thirties: 'Fu lui a prestarmi il primo libro che ho letto di Dos Passos, *Il 42esimo parallelo*' (xxv) [It was he who loaned me the first Dos Passos book I read, *The 42nd Parallel*].

2. The Death of the Detective in *Il cavaliere e la morte*

1 See Caillois, 3, for this definition of the value of the detective novel.

2 See Del Monte, 14, for a discussion of the *romanzo poliziesco* and its origins in the eighteenth century as an expression of the conflict between rationality and irrationality. Whether this theory of origins is historically valid, the detective story as a *forma mentis* certainly belongs to the Enlightenment. Several of Sciascia's fictional detectives – Captain Bellodi of *Il giorno della civetta*; Di Blasi, the Jacobin lawyer of *Il consiglio d'Egitto*; and Inspector Rogas of *Il contesto* – derive their ideals from the *siècle des lumières*.

3 Sciascia cited his affinity for the French Enlightenment as one of the common denominators between his work and that of Calvino: 'Per mio conto credo che Calvino ed io abbiamo in comune il Settecento, il Settecento francese, cioè gli illuministi, Voltaire' [As far as I'm concerned, I believe that Calvino and I have the eighteenth century in common, the French eighteenth century, the Enlightenment thinkers, Voltaire] (see Baldwin's interview with Sciascia, 122).

4 See Cannon, 'The Detective Fiction of Leonardo Sciascia,' for an analysis of Sciascia's increasing departure from the norms of detective fiction as a reflection of the author's decreasing faith in the power of reason. The focus of the article is on *Il giorno della civetta*, *A ciascuno il suo*, and *Il contesto*. See also Cannon, '*Todo modo* and the Enlightened Hero of Leonardo Sciasica.' In *The Doomed Detective* Tani classifies Sciascia's fiction as anti-detective novels, in which the detective novel plot is adapted to 'paint a critical portrait of the sad state of Sicilian (and, generally, Italian) affairs' (54).

5 As Farrell has noted, *Il contesto* lacks any precise geographical settings or references to topical events that would identify the society criticized in the

novel as Italy (84). Yet the context out of which the novel emerged was, as the author himself explained, the occasion of the *compromesso storico*, the historic compromise of the early 1970s between the Italian Communist Party, the Socialist Party, and the Christian Democratic Party. See Ginsborg, 354–8, for a discussion of the events leading to the historic compromise, the role of the Communist leader, Berlinguer, and the flaws inherent in the compromise. The *compromesso storico* was much despised by Sciascia for the way in which all ideological distinctions were blurred beyond recognition. See Cannon, 'The Detective Fiction of Leonardo Sciascia,' 531, and Farrell, 83–92, for a discussion of the political context in which the novel emerged.

6 See Barzun for an analysis of the appeal of the detective genre.
7 Sciascia's thwarting of the reader's expectations places this novel in the category of what Stefano Tani describes as an 'anti-detective novel.'
8 Farrell suggests that, although Sciascia's civic commitment was strong, he was 'paralyzed by his innate pessimism' (9).
9 The equation *sicilianità* = pessimism is one that runs throughout Sciascia's work, beginning with *Le parrocchie di Regalpetra*. In the authorial preface to his first book, Sciascia writes: 'Tutti i miei libri in effetti ne fanno uno. Un libro sulla Sicilia che tocca i punti dolenti del passato e del presente e che viene ad articolarsi come la storia di una continua sconfitta della ragione' (*Opere*, 1:5) [All my books in effect constitute one book. A book on Sicily that touches the sore spots of the past and of the present and that unfolds as the continuous defeat of reason]. On the question of Sicily and *sicilianità*, see Farrell, 32–40.
10 An incomplete list of the authors cited in just a portion of *Nero su nero* includes Proust, Pirandello, Stendhal, Manzoni, Conrad, Voltaire, Malraux, Chesterton, and Petrarch.
11 See Barzun and Taylor, 5, as quoted in Holquist, 154.
12 In *Il nome della rosa* William of Baskerville informs his pupil, Adso, that books do not necessarily speak of things but of books: 'Spesso i libri parlano di altri libri' (288) [Often books speak of other books]. Taking William's lesson to heart, Adso perceives the library as 'un luogo di un lungo e secolare susurro, di un dialogo impercettibile tra pergamena e pergamena (289) [the place of a long, centuries-old murmering, an imperceptible dialogue between one parchment and another].
13 The belief in the power of the pen to function as a sword, a weapon in defense of 'il mondo offeso,' is as old as literature itself. Perhaps the most eloquent spokesman for this view in twentieth-century Italian literature is Elio Vittorini. Vittorini's *Conversazione in Sicilia*, published in the last years of the fascist regime in Italy, portrays writing as a call to arms to right the wrongs of the world.

3. In Search of Isolina

1. Most of the early reviews of *Isolina* refer to the text as a novel. In a 1985 interview Dacia Maraini took pains to distinguish her recently published book from a novel: 'Non è un romanzo ma un racconto che si ispira al vero' (Debenedetti).
2. In his essay 'Storia della colonna infame' Sciascia, borrowing from an article by Renzo Negri, uses the term *inchiesta* to describe Manzoni's text. Sciascia concurs with Negri that *Storia della colonna infame* prefigures a new genre: the '*racconto-inchiesta*.' Maraini's *Isolina* is very faithful to this Manzonian genre, as filtered through Leonardo Sciascia. See 'Storia della colonna infame,' *Opere*, 2:1078–9.
3. See Robin Winks, 'The Historian as Detective,' for an analysis of the similarities between historical discourse and the detective genre. As Winks has pointed out, the *modus operandi* of the historian is remarkably similar to that of the detective: 'The historian must collect, interpret, and then explain his evidence by methods which are not greatly different from those techniques employed by the detective, or at least by the detective of fiction' (242).
4. In 'Oltre e dietro il pudore' Sapegno has pointed out one of the most characteristic features of Maraini's oeuvre: 'ci troviamo di fronte a un occhio di donna sul mondo' (41) [we find ourselves facing a women's eye on the world]. In her astute and perceptive analysis, Sapegno characterizes the point of view constructed by all of Maraini's texts as 'un atteggiamento di ricerca' [an attitude of research]. Sapegno continues: 'la storia che si racconta è ... il frutto di una curiosità inesauribile, di domande a cose e persone, dello scavare e scrutare per rintracciare i fili di una vicenda ... La voce che narra, insomma fa entrare il lettore/la lettrice nel testo dando la sensazione di ... metter assieme via via i pezzi di un puzzle' (42–3) [the story that is told is ... the fruit of an inexhaustible curiosity, of questions posed to people and things, of excavating and scrutinizing in order to trace the threads of a case ... the narrating voice allows the reader to enter into the text, giving the reader the impression of putting together with the author the pieces of the puzzle]. This description of Maraini's *oeuvre* is a particularly accurate portrait of the narrating presence in *Isolina*.
5. This dual structure characterizes the detective novel. As Todorov has pointed out, 'in their purest form, these two stories have no point in common ... The first story, that of the crime, ends before the second begins. But what happens in the second? Not much. The characters of the second story do not act, they learn' (43).

6 See Leonardo Sciascia, introduction to *La Colonna infame: Alessandro Manzoni* (Bologna: Capelli Editore, 1973).
7 For further discussion of Sciascia's debt to Manzoni, see Cannon, *Postmodern Italian Fiction*, 42–4.
8 Maraini regularly runs workshops for creative writers. See *Amata scrittura* for an overview of how the author conducts her literary 'laboratories.'
9 Merry calls *Isolina* 'a forceful study of the invisibilization of women in Italy' (221).
10 In his discussion of historical discourse, Barthes notes that 'objectivity, or the absence of any clues to the narrator, turns out to be a particular form of fiction' (149).
11 As a public intellectual who occasionally resorts to reportage, Maraini herself firmly believes in the power of the press when used in a socially responsible manner. Both the positive and the negative sides of journalism are highlighted in *Isolina*. The author repeatedly calls attention to the biases of the various newspapers reporting on the case. Whatever their stripe, all at some point sensationalize and distort the case while exploiting the victim. In Maraini's *Voci*, the same dichotomy between ethically responsible journalism and tabloid journalism becomes evident. There is a fine line between the investigative journalism in which Michela is engaged in her report on crimes against women and the tabloid coverage of the Angela Bari case. Similarly, both Sciascia and Tabucchi show the positive and the negative sides of journalism in the works studied in this volume.
12 White reminds us in 'Interpretation in History' that this perception of history originates with the major nineteenth-century historiographers, Hegel, Nietzsche, Croce, and Droysen.
13 As Carol Lazzaro-Weis has pointed out in Russell's bibliography of Italian women writers, 'How society victimizes, mutilates, and eventually destroys women by defining female sensuality as immoral in order to excuse crimes against them is powerfully demonstrated in *Isolina*' (219).
14 See Merry, 221, on the 'invisibilization' of women.
15 In *Morte dell'Inquisitore* Sciascia similarly indicts the inquisitors in the Fra Diego La Matina trial: 'E una delle più atroci e allucinanti scene che l'intolleranza umana abbia mai rappresentato. E come questi nove uomini pieni di dotrina teologica e morale ... restano nella storia del disonore umano, Diego la Matina afferma la dignità e l'onore dell'uomo' (*Opere*, 1:685) [This is one of the most atrocious and hallucinatory scenes ever portrayed by human intolerance, and as these nine men, so full of theological and moral

doctrine ... belong to the history of human dishonor, so Diego la Matina affirms the dignity and honor of man] (49).

4. *Voci* and the Conventions of the *Giallo*

1 Maraini's *Voci* can be situated in the broader context of the use of the detective genre by Italian women writers. In *From Margins to Mainstream* Lazzaro-Weis shows how women writers 'exploit the more rigid and codified conventions of detective and crime novels, genres often considered to be antagonistic toward women in general, to express their gendered viewpoints on the form's inherent themes' (xvi). Lazzaro-Weis focuses on the works of two feminist Italian women writers, Cagnoni and La Spina.
2 See W.H. Auden, 'The Guilty Vicarage,' for a discussion of this element of classical detective fiction.
3 See Todorov, *The Poetics of Prose*, 43, on the dual nature of the detective novel.
4 In the classical detective story that reached its heyday in the thirties, the rules of the genre were rigidly codified and vigorously enforced. One of S.S. Van Dine's 'Twenty Rules for Writing Detective Stories' ('There simply must be a corpse in a detective novel and the deader the corpse the better' [as quoted in Lehman, 47]) lays bare the playfulness with which the victim is treated in the classical *giallo*. See Lehman, 45–9, for an illuminating discussion of this element of detective fiction.
5 Klein argues that the difficulty encountered by these writers reflects 'the extraordinary power of the patriarchal script' (4).
6 See Teresa de Lauretis's introductory essay to *Sexual Difference: A Theory of Social-Symbolic Practice* for an analysis of *affidamento* and the *madre simbolica* as articulated by Italian feminists.
7 Testaferri has also remarked on the recurrence of the qualifier *imbranata* to describe Michela: 'In the book this chauvinist cliché becomes an ironic badge of the feminine' (55, n. 10).
8 See Lehman, chapter 9, on the theme of the double in detective fiction. See also Priestman, 50–5.
9 See Ada Testaferri for a perceptive analysis of the *doppelgänger* motif in *Voci*.
10 In *La lunga vita di Marianna Ucrìa*, for example, the uncle's violation of Marianna and the father's tacit consent act as a master metaphor reflecting the violation of women by patriarchy. See my 'Rewriting the Female Destiny' for a discussion of Maraini's treatment of female subjugation within patriarchy in *La lunga vita di Marianna Ucrìa*.

11 The question of how much of male aggression and rape are 'natural' or adaptive behaviour is a timely issue, hotly debated by evolutionary biologists and social scientists. See, for example, Smuts's 'Male Aggression against Women: An Evolutionary Perspective.'

5. Ethics and Literature in *Sostiene Pereira: Una testimonianza*

1 As Klopp points out in 'Antonio Tabucchi: Postmodern Catholic Writer,' 'if the attention devoted to Tabucchi has focused on his postmodernism, what has perhaps not received sufficient notice is the specifically ethical nature of the themes that run through his books' (332).
2 Joseph Francese notes in reference to another of Tabucchi's texts, *I volatili del Beato Angelico*, that 'Tabucchi non accetta la passività del maturo Montale dinanzi agli avvenimenti' (19) [Tabucchi does not accept the passivity of the mature Montale before the world]. Pereira's conversion from passive observer to active participant is another example of what Francese identifies in Tabucchi's prose as 'un diverso modo di intendere la funzione sociale dello scrittore e della letteratura' (19) [a different way of understanding the social function of the writer and of literature].
3 In *Sogni di sogni* Tabucchi imagines the dreams of twenty writers, including Ovid, Rabelais, Rimbaud, Garcia Lorca, Mayakovsky, and, of course, Fernando Pessoa.
4 In the introduction to a special issue of *Annali d'italianistica* devoted to ethics and literature, Cervigni draws upon Wayne Booth while making the point that 'the interplay of literature, criticism and ethics has always been present in Italy's literary culture' (9).
5 For a detailed discussion of the ethics of reading and listening, see Booth, *Company*, 7.
6 In a sustained and perceptive reading of the novel, Brizio-Skov remarks, 'Never for a moment is the reader allowed to forget that the story is the exact transcription of Pereira's words ... the viewpoint offered to the reader is limited ... restricted to what the protagonist himself wishes to reveal, given that the transcriber merely records what Pereira states' (*Sostiene Pereira*, 187).
7 See 'Antonio Tabucchi: Postmodern Catholic Writer,' 331, for this reading of the context in which Pereira provides his testimony.
8 See Ferraro, 163.
9 See Bernardelli, 141, for this latter interpretation.
10 The name *Pereira* is taken from T.S. Eliot's 'Fragment of a Prologue,' in which two friends, Dusty and Doris, discuss a mysterious Portuguese gentlemen named Pereira about whom they know next to nothing. As

Jansen has pointed out, the one aspect of Pereira's character about which they speculate is his trustworthiness: 'What about Pereira? He's no gentleman, Pereira: You can't trust him,' says Doris (115). Jansen suggests that Tabucchi's Pereira, in contrast to Eliot's, offers the words 'sostiene Pereira' as 'a frame to contain the story and the condition to make it trustworthy' (203).

11 See Lopez, 'Antonio Tabucchi: A Committed Doubter,' for Tabucchi's reference to this Council of Europe report.

12 *Sostiene Pereira: Una testimonianza* has been read by many critics as a novel that raises the issue of 'impegno' [commitment]. One of the first reviewers, Coletti, welcomed Tabucchi's 1994 novel as heralding a turn away from the 'letteraria e raffinata' and towards 'una tematica più impegnata.' Bruno Ferraro recognizes in Tabucchi's novel a strong sense of 'impegno civile e politico.' As I have pointed out in the introduction to this volume, there are notable differences between 'la letteratura impegnata' of the immediate post–World War II period and Tabucchi's recent work. Tabucchi himself adopts a distance from the label 'impegnato.' In *La gastrite di Platone* he characterizes the term as follows: 'Termine assolutamente innoportuno, che io non ho mai utilizzato, e che in Italia provoca disgusto immediato' (52). It is more accurate to describe the author's recent work, particularly *Sostiene Pereira* and *La testa perduta di Damasceno Monteiro*, as moving in an ethical rather than a politically committed direction.

6. Detection, Activism, and Writing in *La testa perduta di Damasceno Monteiro*

1 As Klopp has pointed out in 'Antonio Tabucchi: Postmodern Catholic Writer,' in both *Notturno indiano* and *Il filo dell'orizzonte* the outcome of the investigation that has occupied the narrator is 'left deliberately mysterious.' Klopp reads this lack of closure as part of the implicit pact between author and reader in Tabucchi's work, and finds that many of 'his works can seem as much epistemological analyses of reading and writing as representations of reality' (331).

2 In the latter category Tabucchi places the detective novels of Leonardo Sciascia first and foremost. See *Conversazione con Antonio Tabucchi: Dove va il romanzo?* 19–20.

3 This, too, runs counter to the norms of the *giallo*. In 'Twenty Rules for Writing Detective Stories,' S.S. Van Dine states as rule number five: 'The culprit must be determined by logical deductions – not by accident or coincidence or unmotivated confession' (190).

4 See Grella, 84–102, for further analysis of the formulaic qualities of the detective novel.
5 The treatment of Alleg at the hands of the French military forces in Algiers was denounced by many French writers, including Jean Paul Sartre, Andre Malraux, Francois Mauriac, and Roger Martin Du Gard.
6 See Brizio-Skov, *Antonio Tabucchi*, 156–7 and 163, for a detailed discussion of Kelsen's philosophy and Bobbio's critique of Kelsen.
7 As Francese has pointed out, Tabucchi considers 'the belief that in order to write, one must ineluctably choose between active participation in the social arena and hermetic withdrawal from life into the realm of literature' (109) to be a false dilemma. See Tabucchi, 'Equivoci senza importanza.'
8 The inspiration for the book came when Tabucchi received two simultaneous requests. He was invited by a German periodical to bear witness to any aspect of contemporary reality for a volume entitled *Dieci scrittori osservano una realtà di fine millennio*. At the same time, a Portuguese-Jewish friend of Tabucchi's involved in a research project on nomadic ethnic minorities asked for Tabucchi's help in penetrating the world of the gypsy camps of Florence.
9 Brizio-Skov identifies three character types in Tabucchi's *La testa perduta di Damasceno Monteiro*: the victims, the intellectuals called upon to defend the victims, and the 'aguzzini' [torturers] (Antonio Tabucchi, 155). She of course places Manolo in the category of the victims.
10 Tabucchi explains in the authorial note that the first lines of Loton's argument belong to Mario Rossi. See Rossi's *Le regole semplici della libertà responsabile*.
11 See Asbel Lopez's interview with Tabucchi for his comment on this report. In the authorial note appended to *La testa perduta*, Tabucchi also acknowledges the importance of the book *Umano Disumano: Commissariati e prigioni nell'Europe di oggi* by Antonio Cassese.
12 Manuela Bertone has argued convincingly that Tabucchi's *La testa perduta di Damasceno Monteiro* must be read not only in a juridical but also in an ethical light. 'Certamente ispirato dalla riflessione filosofica di Emmanuel Levinas (e pensiamo naturalmente al Levinas pensatore del 'face-à-face') Tabucchi fa del volto il fondamento delle spazio relazionale, stabilendovi il luogo originario della giustizia' (122) [Without a doubt inspired by the philosophical reflection of Emmanuel Levinas (and we are naturally thinking of Levinas as the theoretician of the face-to-face relation) Tabucchi makes the face the foundation of relational space, establishing it as the original seat of justice].
13 Jeannet suggests that, on the one hand, the defective tape recording 'under-

lines the reporter's imperfect comprehension of the lawyer's thought; on the other hand, those fragments point to the difficulty of articulating a coherent discourse about justice and opening up a higher vision of it, in the face of the actual state of human affairs' (165).

14 Spunta has pointed out that ellipsis and reticence are an intrinsic part of Tabucchi's work. She contrasts ellipsis, in which the omissions are not essential for textual cohesion, with reticence, in which information is obscured. In both cases, Spunta suggests, 'Tabucchi employs such discourse structure, and in particular the figures of ellipsis and reticence ... in order to involve the reader in decoding the texts' (104).

15 In his 1984 *The Doomed Detective*, Stefano Tani defines the anti-detective novel as one that stresses social criticism and solutions in which justice does not prevail. Brizio-Skov also reads *La testa perduta* as an anti-detective novel, arguing that it is more faithful to the hard-boiled American tradition than to the classical, English tradition of the detective story. I, instead, find many elements of the classical English detective story in Tabucchi's novel, including the erudition and eccentricity of the detective, Loton's use of armchair detection, and the obvious reference to the Sherlock Holmes–Watson relationship in the interaction between Loton and Firmino.

Conclusion

1 See, for example, Brizio-Skov, *Antonio Tabucchi: Navigazioni in un arcipelago narrativo*, and Klopp, 'Antonio Tabucchi: Postmodern Catholic Writer.' In an interview with Gumpert Melgosa, however, Tabucchi observes: 'Non so se sono proprio d'accordo con l'essere definito un autore postmoderno' (89) [I don't know whether I am fully in agreement with being called a postmodern writer].

2 See Ceserani for further discussion of Tabucchi as a postmodern writer.

3 See *La gastrite di Platone* for Tabucchi's passionate defence of the writer's active and positive role in society.

4 In *The Pleasure of Writing* (ed. Diaconescu-Blumenfeld and Testaferri), Maraini has paid special tribute to 'those extraordinary women like Anna Maria Ortese, Elsa Morante, Lalla Romano, Anna Banti, Natalia Ginzburg, who have taught us to write as women' (25).

5 See *The Pleasure of Writing* (ed. Diaconescu-Blumenfeld and Testaferri), an edited volume dedicated to Maraini's *oeuvre*. The volume both chronicles the author's exclusion from the canon and makes the case for the enduring value of Maraini's work.

6 The Camilleri case is a particularly interesting one. In his introduction to Camilleri's collected detective stories, *Storie di Montalbano*, Borsellino notes that the ever-increasing popularity of the Montalbano stories is inversely proportional to the critical neglect of Camilleri for much of his career. This situation is finally beginning to be addressed. Following his *mea culpa*, Borsellino provides a perceptive and detailed analysis of Camilleri's work and his affinity with some of Italy's greatest writers, from Manzoni, Svevo, and Gadda to fellow Sicilians Pirandello, Brancati, and Sciascia. Borsellino notes many points of contact between Sciascia's work and Camilleri's. He also points out that Camilleri has never exercised the same function in Italian society as a writer like Leonardo Sciascia: 'Camilleri non ha esercitato nei confronti delle vicende italiane la stessa funzione di coscienza critica permanentemente attiva che ha esercitato Leonardo Sciascia' (xxii) [Camilleri has not exercised the same function of a permanently active critical conscience on Italian affairs that Leonardo Sciascia has played]. See also the 2004 Sellerio volume *Il caso Camilleri: Letteraturea e storia*. This edited volume contains essays on Camilleri's Montalbano stories, as well as studies of his historical novels and his less well known but fascinating texts in the tradition of the *racconto-inchiesta*.
7 See Baranski for a perceptive and informative overview of Vassalli's career. As the author points out, except as regards women writers, few authors of the 1980s and 1990s demonstrated allegiance to this view of the social responsibility of literature. Baranski includes Fortini, Sanguineti, Sciascia, and Volponi in this group. I would add Maraini and Tabucchi to this list.
8 See 'The Roots of Torture,' *Newsweek*, 24 May 2004, for a graphic and disturbing description of the inhumane treatment of Iraqi prisoners in Abu Ghraib. The article describes the scene as members of the U.S. Congress watched a three-hour show including eighteen hundred slides and several videos: 'As a small group of legislators watched the images flash by in a small, darkened room in the Rayburn Building ... a sickened silence descended ... The nightmarish images showed American soldiers at Abu Ghraib Prison forcing Iraqis to masturbate, American soldiers sexually assaulting Iraqis with chemical light sticks. American soldiers laughing over dead Iraqis whose bodies had been abused and mutilated' (26). Recent reports suggest that the FBI has uncovered evidence of similar humiliation and sexual abuse of Iraqi detainees in Guantanamo Bay. These reports have come from 'conscience-stricken agents troubled by what they had witnessed.' See 'Unanswered Questions,' *Newsweek* 17 January 2005.

Bibliography

Adamo, Liborio. *Leonardo Sciascia tra impegno e letteratura*. Enna: Papiro Editrice, 1992.
Agnew, John. *Place and Politics in Modern Italy*. Chicago: University of Chicago Press, 2002.
Alleg, Henri. *The Question*. New York: George Braziller, 1958.
Ambroise, Claude. *Invito alla lettura di Sciascia*. Milan: Mursia, 1974.
– 'Verità e scrittura.' In *Leonardo Sciascia Opere*, vol. 1. Milan: Bompiani, 1987, xvii–xxxix.
Anderlini, Serena. 'Prolegomena for a Feminist Dramaturgy of Feminine: An Interview with Dacia Maraini.' *diacritics* 21, nos. 2–3 (1991): 148–60.
Arvigo, Tiziana. 'La narrativa italiana degli anni Novanta.' *Nuova corrente* 44 (1997): 377–413.
Auden, W.H. 'The Guilty Vicarage.' In *Detective Fiction: A Collection of Critical Essays*, ed. Robin Winks. Woodstock, NY: Foul Play Press, 1980.
Baranski, Zygmunt. 'Sebastiano Vassalli: Literary Lives.' In *The New Italian Novel*, ed. Zygmunt Baranski and Lino Pertile. Edinburgh: Edinburgh University Press, 1993.
Barry, John, Michael Hirsch, and Michael Isikoff. 'The Roots of Torture.' *Newsweek*, 24 May 2004, 26.
Barthes, Roland. 'Historical Discourse.' In *Introduction to Structuralism*, ed. Michael Lane. New York: Basic Books, 1970.
Barzun, Jacques. *The Delights of Detection*. New York: Criterion Books, 1961.
Beccaria, Cesare. *Dei delitti e delle pene, Con una raccolta di lettere e documenti relativi alla nascita dell'opera e alla sua fortuna nell'Europa del Settecento*. Ed. F. Venturi. Turin: Einaudi, 1965.
Bellesia, Giovanna. 'Variations on a Theme: Violence against Women in the Writings of Dacia Maraini.' In *The Pleasure of Writing: Critical Essays on Dacia*

Maraini, ed. Rodica Diaconescu-Blumenfeld and Ada Testaferri. West Lafayette, IN: Purdue University Press, 2000.

Bernardelli, Andrea. 'Sostiene Tabucchi. *Quaderni d'italianistica* 21, no. 1 (2000): 137–48.

Bertone, Manuela. 'Tabucchi istruisce il caso Damasceno Monteiro,' *Cahiers du Cercic* 23 (2000): 109–25.

Bobbio, Norberto. *Profilo ideologico del '900*. Milan: Garzanti, 1990.

Booth, Wayne. *The Company We Keep: An Ethics of Fiction*. Berkeley: University of California Press, 1988.

– *The Rhetoric of Fiction*. Chicago: University of Chicago Press, 1961.

Borsellino, Nino. 'Camilleri gran tragediatore.' Introduction to *Andrea Camilleri: Storie di Montalbano*. Milan: Mondadori, 2002.

Brizio-Skov, Flavia. *Antonio Tabucchi: Navigazioni in un arcipelago narrativo*. Cosenza: Pellegrini Editore, 2002.

– '*Sostiene Pereira*: The Crisis of the Intellectual between History and Literature.' *Spunti e Ricerche* 12 (1996–7): 186–201.

Buell, Lawrence. 'In Pursuit of Ethics.' *PMLA* 114 (January 1999): 7–19.

Bufacchi, Vittorio, and Simon Burgess eds. *Italy since 1989: Events and Interpretations*. New York: Palgrave, 2001.

Burns, Jennifer. *Fragments of Impegno: Interpretations of Commitment in Contemporary Italian Narrative, 1980–2000*. Leeds: Northern University Press, 2001.

Buttita, Antonio, ed. *Il caso Camilleri: Letteratura e storia*. Palermo: Sellerio, 2004.

Caillois, Roger. 'The Detective Novel as Game.' In *The Poetics of Murder*, ed. Glenn Most and William W. Stowe. San Diego: Harcourt Brace Jovanovich, 1983.

Calvino, Italo. *If on a Winter's Night a Traveler*. Trans. William Weaver. New York: Harcourt Brace Jovanovich, 1989.

– *Il sentiero dei nidi di ragno*. Turin: Einaudi, 1947.

– *Se una notte d'inverno un viaggiatore*. Turin: Einaudi, 1979.

Cannon, JoAnn. 'The Detective Fiction of Leonardo Sciacscia.' *Modern Fiction Studies* 29 (Autumn 1983): 523–34.

– *Postmodern Italian Fiction: The Crisis of Reason in Calvino, Eco, Sciascia, Malerba*. Rutherford: Associated University Presses, 1989.

– 'Rewriting the Female Destiny: Dacia Maraini's *La lunga vita di Marianna Ucrìa*.' *Symposium* 49 (Summer 1995): 136–47.

– *Todo modo* and the Enlightened Hero of Leonardo Sciascia.' *Symposium* 35 (Winter 1981–2): 282–91.

Cassese, Antonio. *Umano-Disumano: Commissariati e prigioni nell'Europa d'oggi*. Bari: Laterza, 1994.

Cattaruzza, Claudio, ed. *Dedica a Antonio Tabucchi*. Pordenone: Associazione Provinciale per la Prosa, 2001.
Cervigni, Dino. 'Literature Criticism Ethics.' *Annali d'italianistica* 19 (2001): 7–24.
Ceserani, Remo. 'Modernity and Postmodernity: A Cultural Change Seen from the Italian Perspective.' *Italica* 71 (1994): 369–84.
Coletti, Vittorio. 'Ripete Tabucchi.' *L'indice dei libri del mese* 5 (May 1994): 10.
Critchley, Simon, and Robert Bernasconi, eds. *The Cambridge Companion to Levinas*. Cambridge: Cambridge University Press, 2002.
Debenedetti, Antonio. 'Povera Isolina, finita in fondo all'Adige.' *Corriere della Sera*, 4 January 1985.
de Lauretis, Teresa. 'The Practice of Sexual Difference and Feminist Thought in Italy: An Introductory Essay.' Introduction to her translation, with Patricia Cicogna, of *Non credere di avere dei diritti*. In *Sexual Difference: A Theory of Social-Symbolic Practice*, ed. Milan Women's Bookstore Collective. Bloomington: Indiana University Press, 1990.
Del Monte, Alberto. *Breve storia del romanzo poliziesco*. Bari: Editori Laterza, 1962.
Diaconescu-Blumenfeld, Rodica, and Ada Testaferri, eds. *The Pleasure of Writing: Critical Essays on Dacia Maraini*. West Lafayette: Purdue University Press, 2000.
Eco, Umberto. *Il nome della rosa*. Milan: Bompiani,1980.
– 'Il primo dovere degli intellettuali: Stare zitti quando non servono a niente.' *Espresso*, 24 April 1997, 192.
Eliot, T.S. *The Complete Poems and Plays of T.S. Eliot*. London: Book Club Associations, 1977.
'The Fall of Montecitorio.' *The Economist*, 20 February 1993, 45.
Farrell, Joseph. *Leonardo Sciascia*. Edinburgh: Edinburgh University Press, 1995.
Felman, Shoshana. 'In an Era of Testimony: Claude Lanzmann's *Shoah*.' *Yale French Studies* 79 (1991): 39–81.
Ferraro, Bruno. 'Letteratura e impegno.' *Narrativa* 8 (July 1995): 157–72.
Francese, Joseph. 'Tabucchi: una conversazione plurivoca.' *Spunti e Ricerche* 6 (1990): 19–34.
Ginsborg, Paul. *A History of Contemporary Italy*. London: Penguin, 1990.
Grella, George. 'The Formal Detective Novel.' In *Detective Fiction: A Collection of Critical Essays*, ed. Robin W. Winks. Woodstock: Foul Play Press, 1980.
Grimond, John. 'Italy: The Odd Country.' *The Economist*, 26 May 1990, 3–15.
Gumpert Melgosa, Carlos. 'La letteratura come enigma ed inquietudine: Una conversazione con Antonio Tabucchi.' Trans. Antonella Talotti. In *Dedica a Antonio Tabucchi*, ed. Claudio Cattaruzza (17–108). Pordenone: Associazione

Provinciale per la Prosa, 2001. (Originally published in Portuguese; subsequent Spanish translation published as *Conversaziones con Antonio Tabucchi* [Barcelona: Editorial Anagrama, 1995].)
Heilbrun, Carolyn. 'Gender and Detective Fiction.' In *The Sleuth and the Scholar: Origins, Evolution, and Current Trends in Detective Fiction*, ed. Barbara Rader and Howard Zettler. New York: Greenwood Press, 1988.
Holquist, Michael. 'Whodunit and Other Questions: Metaphysical Detective Stories in Postwar Fiction.' In *The Poetics of Murder*, ed. Glenn Most and William Stowe. New York: Harcourt Brace Jovanovich,1983.
Isikoff, Michael. 'Unanswered Questions.' *Newsweek*, 17 January 2005, 36.
'Italy: The Odd Country.' *The Economist*, 26 May 1990, 3–15.
Jansen, Monica. 'What About Pereira? Can He Be Trusted?' *Spunti e Ricerche* 12 (1996–7): 202–14.
Jeannet, Angela. 'A Matter of Injustice: Violence and Death in Antonio Tabucchi.' *Annali d'italianistica* 19 (2001): 153–69.
Klein, Kathleen Gregory. *The Woman Detective: Gender and Genre*. Urbana: University of Illinois Press, 1988.
Klopp, Charles. 'Antonio Tabucchi: Postmodern Catholic Writer.' *World Literature Today*, 71, no. 2 (1997): 331–4.
– 'The Return of the Spiritual, with a Note on the Fiction of Bufalino, Tabucchi, and Celati.' *Annali d'italianistica* 19 (2001): 93–102.
Lazzaro-Weis, Carol. *From Margins to Mainstream: Feminism and Fictional Modes in Italian Women's Writing, 1968–1990*. Philadelphia: University of Pennsylvania Press,1993.
– 'From Margins to Mainstream: Some Perspectives on Women and Literature in Italy in the 1980s.' In *Contemporary Women Writers in Italy: A Modern Renaissance*, ed. Santo Aricò. Amherst: University of Massachusetts Press, 1990.
Lehman, David. *The Perfect Murder: A Study in Detection*. New York: Free Press, 1989.
Levinas, Emmanuel. *Totality and Infinity: An Essay on Exteriority*. Trans. Alphonso Lingis. Pittsburgh: Duquesne University Press, 1969.
London, Artur. *The Confession*. Trans. Alastair Hamilton. New York: Morrow, 1970.
Lopez, Asbel. 'Tabucchi: A Committed Doubter.' Interview with Antonio Tabucchi. *Unesco Courier*, November 1999, 46–50.
Lukàcs, George. *The Historical Novel*. London: Peregrine, 1964.
– *History and Class Consciousness: Studies in Marxist Dialectics*. Trans. Rodney Livingstone. London: Merlin Press, 1971.
Lupo, Salvatore. *Il caso Camilleri: Letteratura e storia*. Palermo: Sellerio, 2004.

Manzoni, Alessandro. *Storia della colonna infame*. Palermo: Sellerio, 1981.
Maraini, Dacia. *Amata scrittura: Laboratorio di analisi, letture, proposte, conversazioni*, ed. Paola Gaglianone. Milan: Biblioteca Universale Rizzoli, 2000.
– *La bionda, la bruna e l'asino*. Milan: Rizzoli, 1987.
– *Buio*. Milan: Rizzoli, 1999.
– *Conversazione con Dacia Maraini: Il piacere di scrivere*, ed. Paola Gaglianone. Rome: Omicron, 1995.
– *Dialogo di una prostituta con un suo cliente*. Padua: Mastrogiacomo, 1978.
– *Donne in guerra*. Turin: Einaudi, 1975.
– *L'età del malessere*. Turin: Einaudi, 1963.
– 'Un giorno Sciascia entrò nella città delle donne.' *L'unità*. 22 november, 1989.
– *Isolina*. Trans. Sian Williams. London: Peter Owens Publishing, 1993.
– *Isolina: La donna tagliata a pezzi*. Milan: Mondadori, 1985.
– *La lunga vita di Marianna Ucria*. Milan: Rizzoli, 1990.
– *Il treno per Helsinki*. Turin: Einaudi, 1984.
– *La vacanza*. Milan: Lerici, 1962.
– *Voci*. Milan: Rizzoli, 1994.
– *Voices*. Trans. Dick Kitto and Elspeth Spottiswood. London: Serpent's Tail, 1997.
Merry, Bruce. *Women in Modern Italian Literature*. North Queensland: James Cook University of North Queensland, 1990.
Milan Women's Bookstore Collective. *Sexual Difference: A Theory of Social-Symbolic Practice*. Trans. Patricia Cicogna and Teresa de Lauretis, with an introductory essay by Teresa de Lauretis. Bloomington: Indiana University Press, 1990.
Morante, Elsa. *La storia*. Turin: Einaudi, 1974.
Mullen, Anne. *Inquisition and Inquiry: Sciascia's Inchiesta*. Leicester: Troubadour, 2000.
Negri, Renzo. 'Il romanzo inchiesta del Manzoni.' *Italianistica* 1 (1972): 14–43.
Novelli, Mauro, ed. *Storie di Montalbano/Andrea Camilleri*. Milan: Mondadori, 2002.
Onofri, Massimo. *Storia di Sciascia*. Bari: Laterza, 1994.
Pertile, Lino. 'The Italian Novel Today: Politics, Language, Literature.' In *The New Italian Novel*, ed. Zygmunt Baranski and Lino Pertile. Edinburgh: Edinburgh University Press, 1993.
Priestman, Martin. *Detective Fiction and Literature: The Figure on the Carpet*. London: Macmillan, 1990.
Ragusa, Olga. 'Alessandro Manzoni and Developments in the Historical Novel.' In *The Italian Novel*, ed. Peter Bondanella and Andrea Ciccarelli. Cambridge: Cambridge University Press, 2003.

Romagnoli, Sergio. '*Dei delitti e delle pene* di Cesare Beccaria.' In *Letteratura Italiana: Le Opere*, II. *Da 500 al 700*, ed. Alberto Asor Rosa. Turin: Einaudi, 1992.

Rossi, Mario. *Le regole semplici della libertà responsabile: La tesi di Mario Rossi*. Venice: Marsilio, 1994.

Russell, Rinaldina. *Italian Women Writers: A Bio-Bibliographical Sourcebook*. Westport, CT: Greenwood Press, 1994.

Sapegno, Maria Serena. 'Oltre e dietro il pudore.' In Dacia Maraini, *Conversazione con Dacia Maraini: Il piacere di scrivere*, ed. Paola Gaglianone. Rome: Omicron, 1995.

Sartre, Jean Paul. 'A Victory.' Introduction to *The Confession*, by Henri Alleg.

Sciascia, Leonardo. *1912 + 1*. Milan: Adelphi, 1986.
- 'Breve storia del romanzo poliziesco.' In Sciascia, *Cruciverba*. Turin: Einaudi, 1983.
- *Il cavaliere e la morte*. Milan: Adelphi, 1988.
- *A ciascuno il suo*. Turin: Einaudi, 1963.
- *Il contesto*. Turin: Einaudi, 1971.
- *Cruciverba*. Turin: Einaudi, 1983.
- *Equal Danger*. Trans. Adrienne Foulke. New York: Harper and Row, 1973.
- *Il giorno della civetta*. Turin: Einaudi, 1961.
- Introduzione. In Sciascia, *La colonna infame di Alessandro Manzoni*. Bologna: Capelli Editore, 1973.
- *The Knight and Death*. Trans. Joseph Farrell and Marie Evans. Manchester: Carcanet Press, 1991.
- *Morte dell'Inquisitore*. Bari: Laterza, 1964.
- *Nero su nero*. Turin: Einaudi, 1979.
- *Open Doors*. Trans. Marie Evans, Joseph Farrell, and Sacha Rabinovitch. New York: Alfred A. Knopf, 1992.
- *Opere*. Vols. 1–3. Ed. Claude Ambroise. Milan: Bompiani, 1987–2002.
- *Le parrocchie di Regalpetra*. Bari: Laterza, 1956.
- *Porte aperte*. Milan: Adelphi, 1987.
- *Salt in the Wound*. Trans. Judith Green. New York: Orion Press, 1969.
- *La scomparsa di Majorana*. Turin: Einaudi, 1975.
- *La sentenza memorabile*. Palermo: Sellerio, 1982.
- *La Sicilia come metafora*. Interview with Marcelle Padovani. Milan: Mondadori, 1979.
- *La strega e il capitano*. Milan: Bompiani, 1986.
- *Todo modo*. Turin: Einaudi, 1974.

Smuts, Barbara. 'Male Aggression against Women: An Evolutionary Perspective.' In *Sex, Power, Conflict: Evolutionary and Feminist Perspectives*, ed. David M. Buss and Neil M. Malamuth. Oxford: Oxford University Press, 1996.

Spunta, Marina. '"Dialoghi mancati": Uses of Silence, Reticence and Ellipsis in the Fiction of Antonio Tabucchi.' *Quaderni d'italianistica* 10, no. 2 (1998): 101–15.

Tabucchi, Antonio. *Conversazione con Antonio Tabucchi: Dove va il romanzo?* Rome: Omicron, 1995.

– 'Equivoci senza importanza.' *Mondo operaio* 12 (December 1985): 109–11.
– *Il filo dell'orizzonte*. Milan: Feltrinelli, 1986.
– *La gastrite di Platone*. Palermo: Sellerio, 1998.
– *Il gioco del rovescio*. Milan: Saggiatore, 1981.
– *The Missing Head of Damasceno Monteiro*. Trans. J.C. Patrick. New York: New Directions, 1999.
– *Notturno indiano*. Palermo: Sellerio, 1984.
– *Pereira Declares*. Trans. Patrick Creagh. New York: New Directions, 1995.
– *Piazza d'Italia*. Milan: Bompiani, 1975.
– *Requiem*. Trans. Sergio Vecchio. Milan: Feltrinelli, 1992.
– *Sogni di sogni*. Palermo: Sellerio, 1992.
– *Sostiene Pereira: Una testimonianza*. Milan: Feltrinelli, 1994.
– *La testa perduta di Damascono Monteiro*. Milan: Feltrinelli, 1997.
– *I volatili del Beato Angelico*. Palermo: Sellerio, 1987.
– *Gli zingari e il Rinascimento: Vivere da Rom a Firenze*. Milan: Feltrinelli, 1999.

Tani, Stefano. *The Doomed Detective*. Edwardsville: Southern Illinois University Press, 1984.

Testaferri, Ada. 'De-tecting *Voci*.' In *The Pleasure of Writing: Critical Essays on Dacia Maraini*, ed. Rodica Diaconescu-Blumenfeld and Ada Testaferri. West Lafayette: Purdue University Press, 2000.

Todorov, Tzvetan. *The Poetics of Prose*. Trans. Richard Howard. Ithaca: Cornell University Press, 1977.

Van Dine, S.S. 'Twenty Rules for Writing Detective Stories.' In *The Art of The Mystery Story*, ed. Howard Haycraft. New York: Simon and Shuster, 1946.

Vassalli, Sebastiano. *La chimera*. Turin: Einaudi, 1990.

Ventavoli, Bruno. 'Voci da un inferno femminile.' *La Stampa*, 22 November 1994, 20.

Vittorini, Elio. *Conversazione in Sicilia*. Turin: Einaudi, 1971.

Waldenfels, Bernhard. 'Levinas and the Face of the Other.' In *The Cambridge Companion to Levinas*, ed. Simon Critchley and Robert Bernasconi. Cambridge: Cambridge University Press, 2002.

White, Hayden. 'Interpretation in History.' *New Literary History* 4 (1973): 281–314.
Winks, Robin. 'The Historian as Detective.' In *Detective Fiction: A Collection of Critical Essays*, ed. Robin Winks. Woodstock: Foul Play Press, 1980.
Wright, Simona. 'Intervista con Dacia Maraini.' *Italian Quarterly* 34, no. 133–4 (1997): 71–91.

Index

Adamo, Liborio, 109n.17
Agnew, John, 110n.24
Alleg, Henri, 93, 96, 120n.5
Ambroise, Claude, 10, 107n.4, 109nn.16,18, 112n.4, 113nn.12,13
Auden, W.H., 117n.2

Balzac, Honore de, 80
Baranski, Zygmunt, 103, 122n.7
Barthes, Roland, 50, 53–4, 116n.10
Barzun, Jacques, 40, 114n.6
Beccaria, Cesare, 22
Bellesia, Giovanna, 108n.5
Bernanos, George, 75, 78–9
Bernardelli, Andrea, 82, 118n.9
Bernasconi, Robert, 22
Bertone, Manuela, 83, 120n.12
Bobbio, Norberto, 120n.6
Booth, Wayne, 76, 77, 112n.10, 118n.4
Borsellino, Nino, 122n.6
Brizio-Skov, Flavia, 108nn.7,15, 109n.19, 118n.6, 120nn.6,9, 121nn.1,15
Buell, Lawrence, 15, 77, 111n.32
Bufacchi, Vittorio, 13
Burgess, Simon, 13
Burns, Jennifer, 110nn.26,27

Caillois, Roger, 113n.1
Calvino, Italo, 110n.28
Camilleri, Camillo, 122n.6
Cannon, JoAnn, 15, 107nn.1,2, 111n.1, 113n.4, 116n.7, 117n.8, 121n.15
Ceserani, Remo, 121n.2
Coletti, Vittorio, 108n.11, 119n.12
Conrad, Joseph: and *The Secret Sharer*, 15, 65
Critchley, Simon, 22, 112n.7

D'Annunzio, Gabriele, 75, 76, 77, 83
Daudet, Alphonse, 8, 80–1
Davis, Nathalie Zemon, 10
death penalty/capital punishment, 5, 18–22, 25, 28–9, 109n.18
Debenedetti, Antonio, 14
de Lauretis, Teresa, 63, 117n.6
Del Monte, Alberto, 113n.2
detective fiction *(giallo)* 3, 10, 15, 31, 35–7, 42, 45, 90, 102–3, 113n.2, 115nn.3,5, 117nn.1–3,4,8, 121n.15; gender/genre relationship in, 61–4; and Maraini, 6, 15, 59–71; and Sciascia, 4–5, 15, 31, 35–7, 42, 102–3, 113n.4, 114n.7; and Tabucchi, 9–10, 15, 87

Diaconescu-Blumenfeld, Rodica, 107n.5, 108n.6, 121nn.4,5
doppelgänger motif, 65, 117n.9
Dostoievsky: *and The Idiot*, 21

Eco, Umberto, 13, 108n.14
Economist, The, 12, 110n.23
Eliot, T.S., 84, 118n.10
Enlightenment, 24, 31, 113nn.2,3
Espresso, 13
ethical: criticism, 75–6, 77, 79–80; nourishment, of reading and writing, 8, 14–15, 26, 27, 43, 79–80, 86, 118n.5; 'ethical turn,' 15, 111n.32
ethically engaged literature 8, 73
ethics: and history, 7, 58; and literature, 7, 8, 15, 73–86, 118n.2

fantastic literature, 7, 84
Farrell, Joseph, 5, 107nn.3,4, 112n.5, 113n.5, 114n.8
fascism, 5, 11, 18, 22, 26, 73, 76, 84–6
Felman, Shoshana, 83
Ferraro, Bruno, 108n.10, 118n.8, 119n.12
focalisateur, 81, 96
Francese, Joseph, 108n.9, 118n.2, 120n.7
freedom of the press, 77–8
futurism, 76

Gadda, Carlo E., 37, 38
Ginsborg, Paul, 114n.5
Ginzburg, Carlo, 10, 109n.15
Giuffredi, Argisto, 22–4
Gogol, Nikolai: *Dead Souls*, 37, 38–9, 41, 43
Grella, George, 90, 120n.4
Grimond, John, 110n.22
Grundnorm theory, 93–4
Gruppo 63, 103, 110n.27

Gumpert Melgosa, Carlos, 85, 111n.29, 121n.1

Heilbrun, Carolyn, 62, 64
historian, 50, 54, 115n.3
historical novels, 10–11, 103, 111n.3
history: as 'constructions,' 55; ethical interpretation of, 7, 58; female, 11–12, 109n.21; perception of, 116n.12; Sciascia's relationship to, 111n.2
Holquist, Michael, 70
human rights violations, 93–4, 96, 97–8, 104–5, 122n.8

incest, 68
Inquisition, 17, 48, 58, 111n.2
interior monologue, 20
investigative: genre *(racconto d'inchiesta)*, 3, 6, 15, 45, 48, 102–3, 115n.2; thrust, 9–10
Italy: political context of study period, 12–14

Jansen, Monica, 83
Jeannet, Angela, 121n.13
journalism, 54, 74, 77–8, 116n.11
justice and injustice, 3–4, 17, 31, 32, 33, 39–40, 42, 48, 57, 58, 99

Kelsen, Hans, 94, 120n.6
Klein, Kathleen, 62, 117n.5
Klopp, Charles, 7, 11, 82–3, 118n.1, 119n.1, 121n.1

Lazzaro-Weis, Carol, 116n.13
Lehman, David, 117nn. 4, 8
Levinas, Emmanuel, 21–2, 112n.7, 120n.12
literary criticism, 91, 92
literature: and ethics, 7, 8, 15, 73–86,

118n.2; fantastic, 7, 84; politically committed literature *(letteratura impegnata),* 13–14, 89, 91, 110n.27, 119n.12; 'rational literature' *(letteratura razionale),* 85; and social responsibility, 103–4, 122n.7; value of, 77, 89, 92, 103–4
London, Artur, 93, 96
Lopez, Asbel, 99, 119n.11, 120n.11
Lorca, Garcia, 8, 15, 75, 77, 83
Lukács, George: *History and Class Consciousness,* 91

Manzoni, Alessandro: *I promessi sposi,* 17, 48, 111nn.1,3; *Storia della colonna infame,* 17, 18, 48, 115n.2
Maraini, Dacia, 3, 4, 6–7, 8–9, 11–12, 13, 14, 45, 50, 52–3, 58, 59, 61, 70, 71, 102, 103, 104, 107n.5, 109n.21, 111n.30, 116nn.8,11, 117n.10, 121nn.4,5; *Amata scrittura,* 51–2; *Bagheria,* 102; *La bionda, la bruna e l'asino,* 109n.21; *Buio,* 59–60, 71, 102; *Conversazione con Dacia Maraina,* 59, 61, 64, 69; *Isolina,* 6–7, 9, 11, 12, 45–58, 71, 115nn.1,2,4, 116nn.9,11,13; *La lunga vita di Marianna Ucrìa,* 6, 11, 68, 117n.10; *Voci* (Voices), 6, 7, 9, 15, 48, 58, 59–71, 116n.11, 117nn.1,9
Maraini, Serena Anderlini, 11–12
Marinetti, F.T., 75, 76–7, 83
Maritain, Jacques, 75, 78
Maupassant, Guy de, 80
Mauriac, Francois, 75, 78
Mayakovsky, Vladimir, 75, 77, 83
Merry, Bruce, 116nn.9,14
metafiction, 4, 15, 103
mise en abîme, 71
monitorial mode, 53–4
Morante, Elsa, 108n.8

Mullen, Anne, 111n.2

narrator: in Maraini's *Isolina,* 115n.5; in Maraini's *Voci,* 60, 63, 66–7, 68; in Sciascia's *Porte aperte,* 19, 20, 24–5, 27–8; in Tabucchi's *Sostiene Pereira,* 81–2
Negri, Renzo, 115n.2
neo-realism, 14, 91, 101, 110n.27
Newsweek, 122n.8

Onofri, Massimo, 112n.5

Pasolini, Pier Paolo, 14
Passos, Dos, 26
Pertile, Lino, 110n.25
pessimism *(sicilianità),* 37
politically committed literature *(letteratura impegnata),* 13–14, 89, 91, 110n.27, 119n.12
postmodernism, 7, 85, 86, 101, 118n.1, 121n.1
post-war period, 89, 91, 92, 101, 110n.27
power, abuse of, 4, 6, 32
power of the pen, 14, 103, 114n.13; and Maraini, 7, 15, 71; and Sciascia, 5, 6, 14, 17–30; and Tabucchi, 80–1, 86, 94
Preistoria, 11–12

'ratiocination,' 45, 67, 69, 88
'rational literature' *(letteratura razionale),* 85
reader, the, 27, 36, 38, 42, 43, 49, 55, 90
reading and rereading, 8, 14–15, 23–4, 27, 37–9, 41, 43, 79–80, 86, 118n.5
reason, 4, 15, 29, 31, 39, 85, 99
romanzo poliziesco, 42, 59, 65, 70, 87, 113n.2

Russell, Rinaldina, 116n.13

Sapegno, Maria Serena, 115n.4
Sartre, Jean Paul, 93
Sciascia, Leonardo, 3, 4–6, 10–11, 14–15, 17, 26, 29, 30, 31, 32, 35–6, 37–9, 42–3, 45, 101, 102–3, 104, 110n.27, 111n.29, 113nn.2,3,5,13, 114nn.7,9; 'Breve storia del romanzo poliziesco,' 31, 34; *Il cavaliere e la morte*, 5–6, 15, 31–43; *A ciascuno il suo*, 4, 17; *Il contesto* (Equal Danger), 4–5, 17, 113n.4; *Il giorno della civetta*, 4, 17, 99; *The Knight and Death*, 33, 35, 36, 37, 40, 41, 42, 43; *Morte dell'Inquisitore*, 10–11, 17, 48, 55, 58, 116n.15; *Nero su nero*, 21, 38, 112nn.8,11, 114n.10; *1912 +1*, 5; *Opere* (Open Doors), 10, 18–30, 33, 34, 35, 36, 37, 40, 41, 42, 43, 109nn.16,18; *Le parrocchie di Regalpetra*, 4, 26, 31, 113n.12, 114n.9; *Porte aperte*, 5, 11, 14–15, 17–30; *La Sicilia come metafora*, 10, 32, 101, 110n.27; 'Storia della colonna infame,' 115n.2; *La strega e il capitano*, 10–11, 14, 17, 111n.30; *Todo modo*, 5, 17
self-reflexiveness, 4, 15, 103
Smuts, Barbara, 118n.11
Spunta, Marina, 121n.14
Stevenson, R.L.: *Treasure Island*, 41, 43

Tabucchi, Antonio, 3, 7–11, 13, 14, 75, 84–6, 87, 95–6, 97, 99, 100, 101–2, 103–4, 110n.27, 118n.1, 120n.8, 121n.1; *Il filo dell'orizzonte*, 87; *La gastrite di Platone*, 14, 110n.27, 121n.3; *Notturno indiano*, 87; *Piazza d'Italia*, 108n.15; *Sogni di sogni*, 75; *Sostiene Pereira* (Pereira Declares), 7–8, 9, 11, 15, 73–86, 119n.12; *La testa perduta di Damasceno Monteiro* (The Missing Head), 8, 15, 46, 87–100, 119n.12, 120nn.8,9,12, 121n.15; *I volatili del Beato Angelico*, 118n.2; *Gli zingari e il Rinascimento*, 94–6
Tani, Stefano, 113n.4, 114n.7, 121n.15
Testaferri, Ada, 107n.5, 108n.6, 117nn.7,9, 121nn.4,5
testimony and judgment, 15, 53–8, 81, 82–4, 85, 86, 96–7
Todorov, Tzvetan, 115n.5, 117n.3
Tolstoy, Leo: *A Confession*, 20–1; *The Death of Ivan Illich*, 32
torture and police brutality, 8, 85, 87, 93–4, 96, 97, 98, 99, 104

Van Dine, S.S., 117n.4, 119n.3
Vassalli, Sebastiano, 122n.7
Ventavoli, Bruno, 107n.5
violence against women, 6–7, 52, 58, 59, 68–71, 107n.5
Vittorini, Elio, 32, 89; *Conversazione in Sicilia*, 3, 32, 39–40, 64, 81, 114n.13

Waldenfels, Bernhard, 21–2, 112n.7
White, Hayden, 7, 55, 58, 116n.12
Winks, Robin, 115n.3
women: female history and memory, 11–12, 109n.21; gender/genre relationship in detective fiction, 61–4; role of victim in patriarchal society, 67, 68–70, 117n.10; violence against, 6–7, 52, 58, 59, 68–71, 107n.5
Wright, Simona, 9, 108n.12
writing: Maraini on cognitive impulse, 8–9, 51, 52; Sciascia on investigative thrust, 9–10; Tabucchi on inspiration for, 9–10